**'You have so much love to give...'
Emma said firmly.**

'No,' Daniel said heavily. 'Love is a myth, a fantasy. It isn't real, it doesn't last.'

She drew back a little. 'You can't believe that. You aren't a loner, not deep down inside. You care too much for other people... I don't believe what you're telling me.'

Daniel's mouth twisted. 'I'm a realist, and I don't get taken in by the illusion of what seems like love.' He grimaced and placed a hand beneath her jaw. 'That doesn't mean we can't be friends, does it?'

D1634429

When **Joanna Neil** discovered Mills & Boon®, her lifelong addiction to reading crystallised into an exciting new career writing medical romances. Her characters are probably the outcome of her varied lifestyle, which includes working as a clerk, typist, nurse and infant teacher. She enjoys dressmaking and cooking at her Leicestershire home. Her family includes a husband, son and daughter, an exuberant yellow Labrador and two slightly crazed cockatiels.

Recent titles by the same author:

TENDER LIAISON

BY
JOANNA NEIL

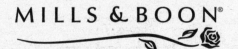
MILLS & BOON®

DID YOU PURCHASE THIS BOOK WITHOUT A COVER?

If you did, you should be aware it is **stolen property** as it was reported *unsold and destroyed* by a retailer. Neither the author nor the publisher has received any payment for this book.

All the characters in this book have no existence outside the imagination of the author, and have no relation whatsoever to anyone bearing the same name or names. They are not even distantly inspired by any individual known or unknown to the author, and all the incidents are pure invention.

All Rights Reserved including the right of reproduction in whole or in part in any form. This edition is published by arrangement with Harlequin Enterprises II B.V. The text of this publication or any part thereof may not be reproduced or transmitted in any form or by any means, electronic or mechanical, including photocopying, recording, storage in an information retrieval system, or otherwise, without the written permission of the publisher.

This book is sold subject to the condition that it shall not, by way of trade or otherwise, be lent, resold, hired out or otherwise circulated without the prior consent of the publisher in any form of binding or cover other than that in which it is published and without a similar condition including this condition being imposed on the subsequent purchaser.

MILLS & BOON and MILLS & BOON with the Rose Device are registered trademarks of the publisher.

First published in Great Britain 1999
Harlequin Mills & Boon Limited,
Eton House, 18-24 Paradise Road, Richmond, Surrey TW9 1SR

© Joanna Neil 1999

ISBN 0 263 81816 0

Set in Times Roman 10½ on 12 pt.
03-9910-53486-D

Printed and bound in Spain
by Litografia Rosés S.A., Barcelona

CHAPTER ONE

'WHAT makes you think you would have the staying power to persevere in this job?' Daniel Maitland frowned and leaned back in his chair, his elbows restlessly nudging the padded leather arms, his hands steepled in front of him.

Emma blinked at the stark question, her lips parting a fraction. His voice was deep and gritty, tingling along her nerve endings in a way that might have been distinctly satisfying under other circumstances, except that he wasn't saying at all what she wanted to hear. She closed her mouth abruptly, uncomfortably aware of him watching her, of the brooding quality of his expression.

Right from the start this interview seemed to have taken a wrong turn, and she wasn't altogether sure of the reason for that. She didn't think she had said or done anything out of place to merit his lack of faith in her. Had he already made up his mind to settle on one of the other candidates?

She shifted a little in her seat, and the ripple of her hair caught the beam of afternoon sunlight that streamed in through the window, burnishing the cloud of chestnut curls with warm hints of gold. His eyes narrowed, following the movement.

'I'm not sure that I understand you properly,' she said evenly. 'Why wouldn't I want to persevere?' Did he imagine she would casually throw away all her years of training? 'I'm a good doctor, and I love my work. It's very important to me.'

He gave her a level look. 'I don't doubt it,' he said, 'but I need someone here who will give my patients a degree of security and stability. I'm not altogether convinced that they'll find it with you, Dr Barnes.'

She looked at him in some confusion, studying his strong, angular features for some clue as to why he was giving her a hard time. He was in his early thirties, she judged, a disturbingly good-looking man, with a clean-cut jaw and compelling dark eyes that were intensely grey, unusual in the way they changed shade with the shifting rays of light.

He was lean and fit, and she guessed he must have considerable drive and self-motivation to be able to command his own practice at such a point in time. From what she had seen so far, he appeared to be aggressively masculine, very confident in what he wanted, and she couldn't imagine him veering off course in any way. Perhaps he simply didn't credit her with the same amount of stamina.

She said carefully, 'I would hope that I could give them both of those things. I've always got on well with the patients in my care—even the difficult ones—and with my colleagues. I really don't foresee any problems that I can't handle.'

His glance was thoughtful, but then he turned his attention to the papers that lay on the polished surface of his desk. 'So far, though, your track record hasn't been particularly good,' he pointed out bluntly, waving a hand broadly over her application form. 'You only worked for six months in a practice where you were expected to stay for much longer, and you went on from there to take up locum work. I'm wondering why you did that. Those don't seem to me to be the actions of someone with long-term career prospects in mind.'

A momentary bleakness came into Emma's eyes and she blinked it away, answering him quietly, 'My sister was ill, and there was no one to take care of her. That's why I gave notice at the practice. I had to put her first and, working as a locum, it meant that I was on hand when she needed me.' She paused, then said on a firmer note, 'Dr Maitland, if you look at my references from the practice, you'll see that there was never any problem as far as my work was concerned. I was doing a good job, and I was happy there. I fitted in. I didn't like having to give it up, and it was just unfortunate the way things turned out and that I had to move on to something different.'

He flashed her a quick, appraising look, then nodded. 'I'm not questioning your references,' he said, more gently this time. 'You wouldn't have been short-listed if they hadn't been first class.' He glanced down at the form once more, before adding, 'This practice is some distance from where you were working before. Do I take it that your sister doesn't need you to look after her any more?'

Emma looked down briefly, her fingers twisting in the fabric of her skirt. She stilled them quickly, smoothing her palms against the fine wool. 'That's right,' she said huskily. He was waiting for her to say more, but she stayed silent, warding off the painful memories that crowded into her head. She couldn't tell him what had happened. Her feelings were still too raw, and she didn't want to risk opening up the wound in front of him.

He looked faintly perplexed, his dark brows edging together. Picking up his pen, he tapped it lightly over the paper, and Emma couldn't help noticing that his hands were strong and capable-looking, his fingers long, the nails blunt-edged. Her gaze travelled to the strong bones of his wrist, and the smattering of dark hair glimpsed from under the crisply laundered cuff of his shirt.

'Why do you want to work here?' he asked. 'This isn't at all like what you've been used to. We're a small-ish community, but the job won't be any easier because of that. There are the outlying villages to think about, as well as the more isolated farms, and in winter time when the snow's thick and the roads are icy they can only add to your problems.'

'I'm not afraid of hard work or bad weather,' she said swiftly. 'I've looked around the area, and I think I can be happy here. It's fairly rural, and clean and fresh, and that's what I want after working in and around the city.'

The Woodhouse practice was reasonably close to where she had been living with Charlotte and little Sophie. Just over a half hour's drive away, which meant she would be able to keep in touch without too much difficulty.

She liked what she had seen of the village and the nearby small town, and she thought that maybe she could settle here. Already she had made the first pay-ment on a small cottage which had appealed to her from the outset. A lot needed doing to it, but that didn't bother her unduly. It would give her something to do, something to take her mind off things.

'You might not feel that way for long,' he remarked drily. 'After being in the city for such a time, the change might come as shock.' From his tone she wondered if he thought that might happen sooner, rather than later, and she studied him thoughtfully for a moment or two.

She really wanted this job. She was right for it, she felt it instinctively, and yet he seemed to be determinedly putting obstacles in the way at every opportunity. His attitude puzzled her.

'Aren't you being a shade too cynical?' she commented. 'What makes you think I would give up so easily?'

'Experience,' he countered laconically, a wry quirk to his mouth. 'I've employed women before who took a fancy to work in the countryside. The novelty wore off pretty soon, and then they started to hanker for the bright lights.' He gave a rueful grimace, then slanted his glance over her once more. His smoke-grey eyes raked her slender figure, flicking over her feminine curves which were outlined by the cotton top she wore beneath her open jacket, and then skimmed back upwards to rest on the oval of her face. Annoyingly, she felt a rush of colour invade her cheeks.

'You're very young,' he said on a faint sigh. 'Much younger than I expected, but maybe I misread your application. You look as though you've just come straight out of medical school.' He shook his head. 'I want someone who will settle in quickly, with the least amount of disturbance to my patients. Someone who would need the minimum amount of supervision, and, as I said before, someone who would provide a reasonable promise of stability. The plain fact is, apart from having a perfectly natural desire for a lively social life, young women have a strong tendency to up and marry and start producing families.'

She lifted a delicately shaped brow at that. 'You can hardly turn me away on those grounds, now, can you?'

He gave a crooked smile. 'Heaven preserve us from the age of political correctness.'

'I can assure you,' she went on stoically, 'I'm perfectly content with my social life as it is, and I've no plans to marry and produce a family just yet. And even though I may look young, I am twenty-eight. Quite old enough to cope with the responsibilities of the medical profession. I can take on my full share of the load from the start, and I can do clinics and minor surgical procedures, which has to be a plus for your patients, surely? After all, who wants to travel to the nearest hospital when they could be dealt with here?'

'There's no argument about your qualifications—they're excellent, and you've presented your case admirably. However…' He paused, sending her a swift, assessing glance, 'I shall need time to think things through. You'll appreciate that I've interviewed several candidates already today.'

He tossed his pen on to the table, then drummed his fingers on the edge of the desk, his thumbs resting on the wooden rim, and she realised he was getting ready to bring the interview to a close. 'I think we've covered most of the issues,' he murmured, 'and there's not a lot more to say for now. If you can bear with me for a few hours, I'll give you a call later to let you know my decision—some time this evening.' He glanced down at his watch. 'Right now, I have to prepare for a surgery.' He pushed back his chair and slanted her a quick smile. 'I do want to thank you for coming here today.'

He stood up in one fluid movement and came around the desk towards her, his long-limbed body supple and full of vibrant energy. He was tall, over six feet, and now that he was close to her she was very much aware that beneath his immaculately tailored suit his body was taut and powerfully muscled. She was acutely conscious of his broad shoulders, hard, flat stomach and strong legs in dark, well-cut trousers.

She got to her feet slowly. She was feeling a little

off balance, and wasn't sure whether it was because the interview was clearly at an end and her future hung in the balance, or because his hand had come to rest lightly on the small of her back as he showed her to the door. It was a simple, natural gesture, but her skin heated unaccountably beneath his palm and she was still tingling fiercely from the brief contact when he opened the door into the reception area and his hand dropped away.

She looked fleetingly around the empty room, gathering her wits. The carpet was deep blue, flecked with grey, and it felt thick and comfortable underfoot. The walls were a fresh cream colour, relieved by the careful placing of framed landscape paintings, and the room was elegantly furnished with chairs upholstered in a restful blue-grey material. There were occasional low, square tables for magazines. In one corner, by the window, there was a children's play area, overlooking a small terrace decorated with tubs of autumn flowers.

The quiet was disturbed by a sudden murmur of voices as a door was opened, and the receptionist hurried towards them, a worried expression on her face. The sound of people talking became clearer, and Emma realised that the tones were subdued and anxious.

'Is something wrong, Alison?' Dr Maitland went to meet the woman, who nodded and seemed to swallow, taking time to compose her thoughts.

'I'm so sorry, Daniel. I was coming to fetch you.' She took a deep breath. 'It's your father. Mrs Harding's just arrived with him. They were on the way to the airport when he collapsed. He's in the treatment room.'

Emma glanced quickly at him. His face had paled slightly at the news, but he went after Alison without breaking his stride, and Emma followed quickly, her senses alert to the signs of distress all around.

His father was lying on the couch in the recovery position, and he didn't seem to be responding to either the nurse who was with him or to the woman who Emma took to be Mrs Harding, a middle-aged woman with greying hair.

He had been sick, and the nurse was replacing the kidney dish with a fresh one while Mrs Harding was gently wiping his face.

Daniel looked at him in concern, then touched his shoulder gently, trying to rouse him. 'Dad, can you hear me?'

There was no intelligible answer, and he checked his father's pupils and his pulse, at the same time asking the woman, 'What happened?'

Mrs Harding's brown eyes were troubled, and she looked as though she was near to tears. 'He insisted he had to go to the hotel in Switzerland, to sort out the problems they are having there. He wanted me to drive him to the airport. I knew he wasn't well enough, but he wouldn't listen. He hasn't seemed himself these last few days, and I thought it was just worry over the business.

'Then, when we were heading out of Woodhouse, he suddenly shouted out and clamped a hand to his head. I didn't know what was happening, but he looked dreadful, and then he seemed to slump, so I turned the car around and brought him here.' Worriedly, she ran a shaky hand through her hair.

Daniel gently squeezed her arm. 'You did the right thing. Thanks.' Then he laid a comforting hand on his father's back, and even though he probably couldn't hear him he muttered quietly, 'We'll take care of you, Dad. Don't worry.'

He turned and spoke to the nurse, acknowledging her

help and adding a few concise instructions, and she went away to quickly set up a trolley. There were lines of strain around his mouth as he went on with his routine checks, swiftly assessing his father's condition.

Emma galvanised herself into action. It looked very much to her as though they were dealing with a CVA—a cerebrovascular accident—due to a blood clot or a haemorrhage, and she felt duty bound to stay on here and help. This was a serious collapse, and they had to act quickly.

'I need an airway—now,' Daniel said.

The nurse appeared with the trolley, and he set about getting the airway in place, inserting the endotracheal tube. Mrs Harding was looking frankly scared so Emma sent her to phone for an ambulance, and the woman hurried away, white-faced but glad to be doing something useful.

Emma wrapped a cuff around the man's arm and checked his blood pressure. After a moment she looked up at Daniel, and said in an undertone, 'His BP's way over the top.'

He nodded. 'We'll have to bring it down.' He frowned, obviously worried about his father's condition, but he continued to monitor his vital signs.

Emma worked quickly to set up an IV line. The poor man was going to need intravenous fluids and special nursing care, along with treatment to reduce any swelling that might occur around the brain.

She and Daniel worked together, co-ordinating their efforts with smooth efficiency. Emma glanced briefly at him. He hadn't hesitated once, had made sure that everything was being done to save his father's life, but he must be deeply shocked.

'The ambulance should be here soon,' she said quietly, her voice soothing and low.

'Moving him could make his condition worse,' he muttered, his expression bleak.

'Do we have a choice? We can only assume it's a subarachnoid haemorrhage, but he needs a CT scan to confirm it and drugs to prevent spasm of the blood vessels as soon as we know for sure. His best chance is hospital. If we can get him stabilised, they can take it from there and do what they can to prevent another bleed.' Further bleeds often happened in the days or weeks after the first, and they could prove fatal.

He let out a long breath. 'You're right, of course. I never expected to find myself in this situation—I've dealt with CVAs so many times, but I never felt like this... I was never in a position where I questioned the next course of action.'

She could understand how he felt. CVAs were unpredictable events, and he would know only too well that his father's life hung in the balance. He looked ashen.

'You've done all you can,' Emma murmured. 'It's bound to be difficult when it's your own family. It's hard to think straight and simply do what you have to do.' She knew that well enough from her own experience.

He must have switched to automatic pilot to get through the last hour, and she felt a growing respect for the way he had acted when under pressure.

Her thoughts were interrupted as the ambulance crew arrived, and Daniel went to meet them and told them swiftly what had happened.

'I want you to keep him absolutely still,' he said to

the paramedic. 'It's imperative there are no sudden jerky movements on the way to hospital.'

'OK.' The man began to supervise the transfer to the waiting ambulance. 'Are you coming along with him?'

'Yes.'

Daniel had already grabbed his medical bag and was following his father outside to the vehicle when he turned and said to Alison, 'Surgery... I almost forgot. See if you can reach Dr Parnell, the locum.'

'He's sick,' Alison said. 'I tried him half an hour ago, and Dr Stanton will be on her way by now and won't be able to get back at a moment's notice. Shall I cancel surgery and divert people to Preston?'

Daniel frowned. 'I'd prefer not to do that if it's at all possible. Ring the standby numbers before you think of cancelling.'

'There's no need to worry.' Emma spoke calmly. 'I'll do it for you. I'm here already, so I may as well make myself useful.'

Daniel sent her a quick glance, his eyes dark, tension showing in the taut lines around his mouth, and she suspected he didn't willingly delegate. She said carefully, 'You know that I've done locum work. I'm used to fitting in.'

'Even so...'

His reluctance was plain enough, and she added, 'This is exactly the sort of situation I've dealt with before.'

'Maybe, but you don't know the set-up here. The patients don't know you.'

'I'll find my way quickly enough. I imagine the notes are all on file and up to date so I won't be working in the dark. I've done this sort of thing many times without any difficulty—my references bear that out. As to the

patients, I dare say they'll adapt easily enough provided
they're forewarned about the situation.'

Slowly, he nodded. 'Are you sure about this? You
shouldn't feel obliged, you know. We are geared up for
crises, but it will take a while to organise something.'

'Of course, I'm sure. Go with your father and forget
about things here. I wasn't planning on going anywhere
for the next week or so, so I can stay for as long as I'm
needed.'

His shoulders relaxed a fraction. 'Thanks,' he murmured. 'It should only be for a short time. And thanks
for all your help back there—you were great.' Then he
turned away, his attention already focused back on his
father.

Emma stood and watched the doors to the ambulance
being closed and waited until the vehicle had pulled
away before she turned and walked back into the building. She hoped things would go well once they reached
the hospital. The next few hours would be critical and,
knowing this, Daniel must be worried sick. He had held
together remarkably well under the circumstances.

'What time is surgery due to start?' she asked Alison,
who looked at her watch and pulled a face.

'In just a few minutes. I can see that people are starting to arrive already. Afternoon patients come in by
appointment, but we do get one or two callers who want
to see if they can be fitted in.'

Emma nodded. 'If you show me where my room will
be, I'll take the time to get accustomed to my surroundings and see how the system works. Just let everyone
know that Dr Maitland is unavailable for the present so
that I don't come as too much of a shock to them.'

'I'll do that.' Alison smiled, relaxing a little now that
things were more organised. 'You can use Dr Stanton's

room, since she'll be away for a while. She's our trainee doctor and she's on a course for the next few weeks.'

Understanding began to dawn on Emma. No wonder Daniel hadn't been keen on someone he thought might be inexperienced. He probably had his work cut out as it was.

They walked along the corridor, then Alison pushed open a door and said, 'This is her base.' Emma glanced briefly around and found that the room was compact, neatly arranged. 'The computer's already set up with the relevant files,' Alison remarked, 'so you shouldn't have too many problems. Just shout if you need anything.'

Emma looked around, noting the screened-off examination area, the washbasin in the corner and the tidy desk. There was a shelf unit on one wall, equipped with up-to-date texts which she recognised.

'I'm sure I'll be fine. Give me a few minutes, though, and then I'll ring for the first patient.'

'Of course. I'll bring you the list. Would you like a cup of tea?'

'Please, that would be lovely.' Emma returned the woman's smile, and when Alison had gone from the room Emma set about examining the contents of the desk drawers for equipment.

The nurse she had worked with earlier put her head round the door. Her short fair hair had been freshly combed and her neat blue uniform was covered with a clean white apron. 'Hi—I'm Jane, the practice nurse. It's great of you to step into the breach like this. I'm on hand to do blood and urine tests and so on, if you need me. If you have any walking wounded, just send them along to me and I'll deal with them. I'll be taking a clinic, but I'm fairly flexible.'

Emma's mouth made a wry shape. 'So I gathered. You did a marvellous job back there. It was a worrying situation but you were very calm and efficient. I only hope the poor man comes through it all right. Did you know him at all?'

'I've met him a few times,' Jane answered. 'He owns the Regency Hotel in town, and I've been to the occasional function there and chatted with him. Daniel thinks the world of his father. John brought him up single-handedly for quite some time, and the bond between them is very strong. I think Daniel was sort of shell-shocked after his mother went, and it made him and his father much closer. Not that he talks about his family life much,' she added hastily, as though she had said too much.

Emma wondered what had happened to his mother. Had she died? Or perhaps there had been a divorce. Either way, it was a sad business, and she found herself wanting to know more, even though she had only met Daniel for the first time today. As it was, the circumstances had hardly lent themselves to getting to know him well, either then or in the future.

Alison arrived with tea and biscuits, and Emma turned her attention to the list of patients as the two women left her alone. She switched on the computer to access the files and skimmed the contents, then rang the bell for her first patient.

The afternoon went smoothly on the whole. Most people were initially wary on coming face to face with a doctor they didn't know, but for the most part they soon accepted the situation.

Tracy Walker, a timid little girl with stomach pains, was Emma's most difficult challenge of the afternoon. Winning her confidence wasn't easy, and it took some time to persuade her to stop crying and relax enough to let Emma examine her, but letting the girl try out the stethoscope helped a lot. The child was fascinated by the experience and after a while she allowed Emma to settle her on the couch.

'Can you tell me where it hurts, Tracy?' Emma asked.

Tracy was pale and slightly underweight, but, after checking her out, Emma concluded that, on the face of it, there didn't seem to be anything to give cause for concern.

The child managed to provide a urine sample, and that proved to be free from infection so Emma decided to delve a little deeper into the situation. You could never tell with children, and tummyaches that came on for no apparent reason when all else seemed fine were best checked out thoroughly.

'How old are you, Tracy?' she asked.

'Five,' the little girl answered, and Emma looked suitably impressed.

'And have you started school?'

Tracy nodded.

'What do you think of it? Do you like it?'

'It's all right.' She shrugged thin shoulders. 'We do pictures and writing, and I play in the home corner.'

'That sounds like fun!'

The little girl nodded again, and from her general attitude Emma reflected that she didn't seem unduly bothered by anything in that area.

Her mother said, 'She started just over a month ago. I think she's settled down well enough, except for the odd day when she's tired and gets out of bed the wrong side.'

'I expect we all have those sorts of days.' Emma

laughed, then added gently, 'I really don't think there's anything to worry about. It may be that she's been having a few painful spasms, but I can give her some medicine to ease that.'

She printed out a prescription and gave Tracy a smily-face sticker from a batch she had found in one of the drawers to press on her jumper as she went out of the door.

Her last patient of the afternoon was a man in his fifties, who looked uncomfortable from the moment he stepped into the room, and gave her the strong impression that he would much rather be somewhere else.

Emma glanced at his notes. 'Hello, Mr Jackson. What can I do for you?'

He shrugged awkwardly. 'It's just this pain I keep getting. Reckon I've pulled a muscle and you could fix me up with a painkiller.'

'Where do you feel the pain?'

Stewart Jackson put his hand over the centre of his ribcage. 'Just here. It feels heavy, like. Fair takes my breath away sometimes.'

'Is the pain there all the time?'

He shook his head. 'It comes and goes. Must have been overdoing it with the digging... I wouldn't have come here—don't hold with being at the doctor's every five minutes—but it's the job, you see. I have to lift things, and it gives me some gyp every now and then.'

Emma scanned his notes fleetingly on screen. From the consultations he'd had with Daniel, it looked as though he'd been suffering from angina, and she needed to check that the problem was being adequately controlled and find out whether this pain really was something different.

'I think I'd better take a look at you,' she murmured, reaching for her stethoscope. 'If you would undo your shirt…'

He did as she asked, and she listened to his chest, asking quietly, 'Show me again where you get the pain. Does it stay in the one place?'

'Goes down my arm sometimes, and in the shoulder. Poor old crock. Falling apart, I am.' He laughed wheezily, then said, 'I told Doc Maitland it was just indigestion, but he went on about tests and suchlike. Wanted to have me wired up, and send me to the hospital. No way…I don't hold with hospitals. I reckon I've gone and done something to the muscles, that's all. Can't you just give me something to get rid of the pain?'

Emma glanced at her screen. 'What medication are you taking at the moment?' she asked.

'I've got some tablets that I'm supposed to dissolve under the tongue but they give me terrible headaches— and some other tablets, but they make my feet feel cold all the while so I don't like taking them unless I really have to. Anyway, I don't hold with tablets.'

Emma smiled and nodded understandingly as she checked his blood pressure. 'I know,' she said, then added on a more serious note, 'The thing is, Mr Jackson, I don't think your problem is indigestion or a pulled muscle. I believe it's a little more complicated than that.' His BP was raised as she had expected. 'You can put your shirt back on,' she told him, going to sit back down at the desk.

When he came back to sit, facing her, she said, 'The trouble is, your blood vessels have probably narrowed over time, and if you do anything at all strenuous the heart has to work that much harder to pump the blood through the smaller space. That can mean that less oxygen gets to the heart and your heart muscles start to complain and cause the pain you're feeling.' She paused, watching his expression to gauge whether he had understood what she was saying.

'Doc Maitland said something about the blood vessels. He put me on a diet, but it doesn't seem to have helped.'

Emma glanced at her screen and saw that Daniel had advised a cholesterol-reducing diet. 'It was probably intended to prevent the condition from getting any worse, as one part of the whole treatment.'

'Oh, well, maybe you're right,' Stewart conceded. 'But I don't get along with the tablets.'

'You could take a smaller dose,' Emma remarked. 'That might help prevent the headaches—or we could see how you get on with a spray that I can give you.' She was concerned that his condition hadn't improved, though it might simply be that he hadn't been taking the medication.

'The way the medicine works,' she explained, 'is that it opens up the blood vessels and allows the blood to flow more easily, which should help to lessen the pain. But I do think Dr Maitland was right and that you really need to go and see a specialist at the hospital…'

From the way he started to fidget, she could see he was about to embark on another 'I don't hold with…' and she tacked on quickly, 'Think of the pain as a warning signal, Mr Jackson. It's telling you that something isn't quite right, and we really need to find out what's happening so that we can get you on the road to recovery. Whatever tests are involved, the doctors and nurses at the hospital will make sure you are comfortable and explain things to you properly. There's no need for you to be worried about it. There are treatments which can make your life so much easier, but we have to assess your condition properly first.'

He was quiet for a minute or two, and she allowed him time to think things through. She had always believed that part of being a good doctor was being able to explain things to the patients properly and then letting them voice their worries.

He pulled a face. 'Well, I suppose if you really think it would be the right thing to do…' he said, doubtfully.

'I do, Mr Jackson. I can get the receptionist to arrange the appointment for you, and we'll hope that you don't have too long to wait.' She looked at him expectantly.

'You and Doc Maitland are two of a kind, aren't you?'

She gave him a crooked smile at that. 'As far as your treatment is concerned, certainly.'

'Oh, all right, then,' he said. 'Might as well see what they've got to say.'

'Good. We'll fix that up. And in the meantime I'll prescribe a spray for you to use whenever the pain comes on.'

He went out of the room a minute or two later, leaving her to add the final details to his notes and then clear her desk. That done, she went through to the office to find out if anything had cropped up in the last half-hour or so.

'There aren't any more people for you to see,' Alison said. 'Jane's referred a patient from her Well-Woman clinic this afternoon to see the doctor. A Mrs Fran Halloway. She'll have gone home by now, though. She had to go and pick up her friend from work so her appointment will have to wait a day or so. As for the rest, I've managed to arrange cover for tonight. Tomorrow might be a problem, though. Daniel phoned-from the hospital, but I can't imagine him being back here for the morning, the way things are.' She ran a hand distractedly through her hair, and Emma glanced briefly over the diary for the next day.

'There's nothing there that I can't handle,' she said. 'Don't worry about it. Was there any news from the hospital?'

Alison shook her head. 'Nothing yet, but Daniel mentioned his father would need some of his things brought in. The only trouble is, I can't get hold of the housekeeper, Mrs Harding. I know she had plans to go and stay with her daughter for a few days, but I don't know if she'll have left already. She said something about a train, though she was thinking about staying on here after what happened. There's nothing that she can do, really, by waiting around, and her daughter's pregnant and having a hard time of it so she'll want to be with her. I expect she'll want to keep in touch, even so.'

'Whereabouts is the house? If it's on my way, I can perhaps call in and see if she's around anywhere. Or maybe she'll have left a key with a neighbour.' Emma wasn't in a great hurry to go home, and added, 'If Mrs Harding can't make it to the hospital, I suppose I could help out. There's no reason why I couldn't pick up what's needed and take it along to the hospital.'

'Are you sure? I don't think Daniel will want to leave his father right now, so it would be a great help.'

Emma nodded. 'Unless he would think I was intruding. I don't want to get in the way.'

'What makes you think that you would? Was he a bit short with you?' Alison pulled a face. 'I wouldn't worry about it. He can be a bit bearish sometimes, but he's lovely really, underneath. He had a bad run-in with a girlfriend once, and it's tended to make him wary. He doesn't take anybody on trust right away, but once he gets to know you and sees that you're on the level, he's great.'

Emma wondered about the girlfriend, but said, 'He was fine…just preoccupied with making the right choice, I think. Anyway, I don't mind helping out. I'd like to see for myself how the man is doing.' Besides, if she was honest with herself, she didn't much feel like going back to a cold, empty house just yet. She would only start to think about Charlotte and Sophie, and how much she missed them. A familiar ache started up inside her and she pulled air into her lungs and shored up her defences. 'How do I get there?'

Alison gave her directions, and after a few minutes Emma set off. The house was about five miles from the surgery, situated in a quiet, tree-lined avenue, set back from the road.

Mrs Harding, she discovered, had just come in from the shops and was about to leave a contact number.

'Bless you for lending a hand,' she said. 'I was wondering what to do.' She fetched a few things from upstairs, then came into the kitchen and started folding pyjamas and towels and wash things into an overnight bag. 'I knew he'd be wanting these, and it was worrying me how to get them there when I'm supposed to be catching my train. My husband is meeting me at the station. It's a terrible business—if it wasn't for the fact that my daughter and my grandchildren are expecting me—'

'Of course you must go and see them,' Emma agreed. 'You'll want to be with them now. If there's any news, I'll phone you there, I promise.'

With that settled, Emma set off for the hospital. It had been an odd, anxious and surprisingly eventful day, but somehow she felt more on top of things than she had in many a month. Perhaps it had served as a turning point, a slow relinquishing of the unhappiness of the past and a gradual embracing of what the future had in store. It was odd, but in a very short space of time she had found herself becoming more and more involved in the lives of the people at Woodhouse. Would she, just as quickly, have to leave them behind?

Daniel hadn't hidden his opinion, that he didn't think she was the right one to join his practice, but she felt a kind of affinity with him all the same. She could only guess at what he must be going through right now, but it must be a lonely and difficult time for him, no matter how well he kept his feelings hidden away.

She had suffered in the same sort of way, when Charlotte had succumbed to illness, and she knew how mind-numbing it could be to stand by and watch and feel helpless. She turned the car towards the city road.

CHAPTER TWO

EMMA arrived at the hospital about an hour later and quickly found the ward where John Maitland was being cared for. She made her way to Sister's office and saw that Daniel was in there, alone. He turned from the window as she opened the door, his grey eyes scanning her slim figure briefly and registering surprise.

'Emma? What are you doing here?' He came towards her and, though his manner was controlled and brisk, she could see the underlying tension in him, the way he held his shoulders stiffly, the strained lines of his face.

'I brought a few things for your father.' She indicated the overnight bag, and set it down on a chair. 'Just a change of clothes, soap, towels, and so on.'

'Thanks. That was thoughtful of you.' He gave her a quick smile. 'But you didn't have to do that, you know. We've imposed on you enough already.'

Emma shrugged. 'It was no trouble. I had nothing planned for this evening and, besides, I wanted to know how your father was doing. Is there any news?'

He grimaced. 'Nothing positive yet. I came in here while the nursing staff are with him. He's had a CT scan, and that showed we were right in our diagnosis. It was a subarachnoid haemorrhage.'

Emma winced at that. The defect had probably been there all his life, a weak place in the blood vessels, which would have eventually ballooned under pressure and then ruptured.

'I'm so sorry.' Impulsively, she put her hand on his

arm in sympathy, knowing that he must still be feeling terribly shocked by what had happened. The simple gesture of human contact was all that she could offer, and she felt oddly helpless.

He acknowledged her touch with a brief slanting of his head but his expression was preoccupied, and after a while she moved her hand away. He said, 'It was an accident waiting to happen. This last high rise in his blood pressure would have been enough to put the finishing touch to a bad scene.'

'Has he always had high blood pressure?'

He shook his head. 'Not always. But lately more so, possibly. He works too hard, drives himself too far, trying to keep up with his business interests, and it was bound to tell on him in the end.'

She nodded. 'I heard that he owns the Regency Hotel in town,' she murmured, 'and I think there was some mention of another in Switzerland. How long has he been in the hotel business?'

'As far back as I can remember—before I was born. He started small and built things up gradually over the years. It was something he had set his heart on, and he's a very determined man. Now he owns a chain of them.' Daniel's mouth tilted fleetingly and pride sparked in his eyes. 'He had very definite ideas about what he wanted, and they all have their own distinctive character…a business or sporting bias, or simply a luxury hotel in beautiful surroundings where people can relax.'

'I suppose he must have done a good deal of travelling in order to keep tabs on what's happening,' Emma said, thoughtfully. 'Was it becoming a strain for him?'

'I imagine so. He doesn't like to talk all that much

about his problems. It's a job getting anything out of him. He just bottles it up inside. The trouble is, he's a workaholic and he doesn't know how to delegate.' A muscle in his jaw moved spasmodically. 'He's going to have to learn now, isn't he? If he comes through this safely.'

Emma wished there was something she could say, or do, to ease what he was going through, but she was a realist, and she knew the only answer for his father lay in the skill of the medical team and the overall success of the practical measures they took. So she said, 'What are they doing now—an infusion to prevent spasm of the blood vessels, along with anti-hypertensive therapy?'

He nodded, and said on a brighter note, 'At least that will give them more time to make a thorough assessment of his condition. The neurosurgical team are considering the best course of action. If he shows some improvement in the next day or so, they might decide to operate, but it all depends on his level of consciousness and the degree of damage that's been done.'

'I know this is a difficult time for you,' Emma said, watching the way his fingers were gripping the back of a chair. 'You've been here for hours, simply waiting for developments. Have you had anything to eat or drink?'

He looked at her blankly, and she persisted, 'It's ages since lunchtime. You ought to have something inside you, if only a cup of coffee and a sandwich.'

'To be honest, I hadn't given it a thought,' he said, sounding faintly surprised. 'I'll get something later.'

'Now would be better,' she persisted. 'The cafeteria will be open for meals, and you need to keep up your strength if you're going to be of any use to your father. We could go over there together, if you like.'

He shook his head. 'I wasn't planning on going anywhere. I want to stay right here until I hear any more news.'

'You, of all people, must know that you could be waiting around for a long time. You'd be better off shoring up your strength with some food. Why don't you come with me? I can leave my pager number for Sister, and she'll bleep us if there's any change. A hot meal will do you the world of good.'

He threw her a look of frank exasperation. 'Emma, I really don't need you to fuss over me like a mother hen,' he told her firmly. 'I don't need any woman flapping around me. My only concern right now is to know what's happening to my father. It may well be a long time before I get to know anything, but I'm in no hurry to go anywhere just yet.'

Faced with his determined refusal, she ought to have been abashed, but she pulled in a deep breath and said, 'OK. I'll bring something up here for you.'

He laughed then, a short, low rumble of sound which was so unexpected that she looked at him in astonishment.

'You're a stubborn little thing, aren't you?' he remarked with a crooked smile, studying her from beneath thick, dark lashes, his gaze wandering over her from head to toe with new interest. 'You simply don't give up. You're slender and willowy, as though a breeze might blow you over at any moment, but underneath...' He paused, a glint lighting the dark eyes. 'Underneath, I suspect there's a thread of pure steel.'

'Well, I'm glad you see it at last,' she murmured. 'You'll realise that I'm not at all used to taking no for an answer.'

'So I gather.' His mouth tilted again at the corners,

making him seem younger somehow and rakishly good-looking. 'You and my father would get along well. He's always been one to tackle problems head on.' He continued to study her leisurely, and a faint heat rose in her cheeks under the deliberate, lingering scrutiny. 'Have *you* eaten since lunchtime?' he asked suddenly.

She thought back, then shook her head. 'Only a cup of tea and a biscuit. There hasn't been time for anything more.'

'Because you were busy taking over for me.' He reached for a notepad and pen. 'Then the least I can do is buy you supper.' He bent slightly to scribble something on the pad, then quirked a brow at her. 'Pager number?'

She gave it to him, and he noted it down, leaving a message for Sister. Then he straightened, and she was conscious once again of how near he was to her, and his aura of powerful masculinity made her feel strangely uncertain for a moment.

'I owe you for the way you helped out today,' Daniel said, taking her arm and ushering her to the door. 'You were brilliant, helping out with my father, and then you were thrown in at the deep end at a moment's notice, taking my surgery. Bless you for all you've done. How did you manage?'

'It was hardly the deep end,' she laughed, protesting. The feel of his hand on her arm was oddly exhilarating, and she had to make herself concentrate on answering his question. 'Everything went just fine. There weren't any real problems. I expect people were just too taken aback to see a new face to do anything but explain their troubles and go out clutching their prescriptions.'

'I'll bet they were.' He grinned. 'It's not every day they come face to face with a flame-haired beauty who looks little more than a teenager and turns out to be their doctor.'

Emma blinked, not sure what to make of that statement, but he was moving swiftly along, and she had to adjust her step to keep up with him.

They reached the cafeteria/restaurant on the ground floor of the hospital, and were lucky enough to find a table next to a window, overlooking the floodlit quadrangle. Emma could just about make out the shrubbery bathed in yellow light and various pieces of stone sculpture partly in shadow.

'So, there was nothing out of the ordinary to cope with this afternoon?' Daniel queried, when they had unloaded their trays onto the table. 'Just the usual symptoms?' He made a wry face. 'Bronchitis, athlete's foot, rheumatics?'

Emma smiled, picking up her fork. The appetising aroma of casseroled vegetables wafted up to her nostrils and made her realise how hungry she was.

'There was a little girl with tummy pains and no apparent cause,' she told him. 'The biggest worry was getting her to relax. Usually I have a crate of toys and puppets and whatnot to hand to help me out with diversionary tactics, but I had to rely on the novelty value of the plain old stethoscope today.' She speared her food and tasted it appreciatively. 'Actually, it probably intrigued her more than anything else might have done.'

'I can imagine.' His eyes crinkled at the corners, and she noted absently how distractingly attractive he was when he relaxed. 'It can be really difficult to know how to assess young children,' he said, 'especially if they're too young to tell you what's wrong—and yet they can be more rewarding than anything else with their liveliness, the chirpy way they talk to you when they're feeling better. Practically at death's door one minute and teasing you the next. They're so resilient.'

He turned his attention momentarily to the pie crust on his plate, then said, 'This is good, very good. You were right—I'm starving.' After a while, he prompted her again, asking, 'Were there any other difficult customers?'

'Only one, who was hoping I'd send him away with a painkiller for a muscle strain, only it wasn't quite as simple as that.' She told him about Stewart Jackson, and he listened carefully, nodding occasionally.

'At least he's agreed to an appointment at the hospital. He's a bright old spark, worked hard all his life and looked after his family, and then suddenly his health started to fail. He's finding it hard to accept. I suspect he's gone into a kind of denial. I've been trying to persuade him for some time now that he needs to have proper tests, but he wouldn't hear of it. He was always coming up with excuses.'

'Doesn't hold with all that fancy equipment,' Emma said, lightly mimicking Stewart's tones, and they both chuckled.

'You must have the magic touch where he's concerned. It looks as though we might be getting somewhere at last.' He smiled at her, looking pleased. 'You did well.'

His praise gave her a warm feeling inside. 'I expect he was just afraid,' she murmured. 'I don't suppose he would have wanted to admit it.'

'Probably not.' He pushed away his plate. 'Has Alison managed to arrange cover for tomorrow?'

Emma shook her head. 'There was no need. I said I would do it.'

He looked at her searchingly. 'It's good of you to say

that, but we shouldn't keep making inroads into your time like this. You have your own life to lead.'

'You're not interrupting anything special.' She thought of the cottage, and the work that needed to be done to make it comfortable. 'Only some renovations to the house I've just bought, and there's no rush to get on with those.'

'Do you have someone to help you with them?' He poured coffee for both of them and paused as she shook her head.

'I live alone. I'm a free agent, so at least I can please myself.'

He raised a dark brow. 'There's no man friend waiting in the wings?' She shook her head and he looked frankly sceptical. 'I find that very hard to believe.'

Her lips quirked. 'Believe it,' she said, digging her spoon into the fruit pudding and moving it about the dish. 'There's no one, so my time's entirely my own.' She said it lightly and turned her attention back to the pudding, but found that her appetite had faded all at once.

The last year had been such a busy one, looking after Charlotte and Sophie, and now all that was behind her there were times when she felt unbearably sad and lonely. It didn't do to mope, though, and she pushed away the dish and reached for her coffee instead, sipping the hot liquid slowly, to give herself time to compose her thoughts.

'So,' she said, after a moment, 'you can take the time to be with your father, and let me look after things back at Woodhouse.' She would be glad of the chance to keep busy. 'You can trust me. If anything crops up that you should know about, I'll ring you, I promise.'

'In that case,' he murmured thoughtfully, 'I think we

should put this on a more formal basis. I'll ask Alison to sort out a paper for you to sign.'

Emma nodded. 'OK. Your other locum is still suffering from a nasty bout of food poisoning, I gather. But I can cover for you for as long as it takes.'

A half-smile tugged at his mouth. 'Thanks, but I was thinking in terms of something rather more permanent than that. You do still want the job, don't you?'

Her blue eyes widened. 'Do I want it?' She laughed. 'Of course I do.' Then she sobered and said more cautiously, 'Are you sure? You seemed to have so many doubts before.'

A line furrowed his brow. 'Are you trying to talk yourself out of it?'

'No, not at all,' she denied vigorously. 'It's just that so much has happened in the last few hours, and you might come to regret making a decision under these troubled circumstances. I'd rather you were absolutely sure, and not feel obligated to me because I was there at the time and able to help out. It wouldn't make for a good working relationship later on.'

Daniel's mouth twisted. 'I don't make decisions on an arbitrary basis. You've coped really well in circumstances that were quite out of the ordinary. As well as that, you managed to talk Stewart Jackson into going into hospital for tests at the first shot, and I'm indebted to you for that.' He sent her a narrowed, assessing glance.

'As to our working relationship, I'm sure we shall manage to get along just fine.' Then, in a more businesslike manner, he added briskly, 'So, we'll get the contract sorted out over the next few days, and you can make a start—officially.'

He glanced over the table at their empty coffee-cups,

and said, 'If you've finished, I'll go back to my father
and let you go on home. It must have been a hard day
for you as well. I won't leave you to cope with everything on your own for long, but I do want to be with
him over the next few hours.'

'I hope things go well for him,' she murmured quietly, and laid her hand over his and squeezed gently.
He was still for a moment, his dark eyes sparking with
something she couldn't quite read, and she wondered
fleetingly if he kept some kind of barrier between himself and the outside world, a protective distance that
denied close, uninhibited contact. Then his fingers
curved around her own, and the warmth of his response
brought a sudden lump to her throat.

Emma left the hospital a short time later, the memory
of that touch still lingering as she drove back to the
cottage. She felt strange after the day's events, as
though something momentous had happened in her life.
A turning point had been reached, and a small inner
glow flamed inside her as she thought about the future.
Things were definitely beginning to look up. She had a
new job, new prospects, and that night she went to bed
with a contented mind for the first time in months, falling asleep almost as soon as her head touched the pillow.

She went into work early next day, refreshed and in-
vigorated, which was just as well because morning surgery turned out to be busier than she had expected, with
the recent bout of cool, damp weather bringing a crop
of wheezy chest complaints and snuffles. She worked
through her list efficiently, allowing a few minutes for
the straightforward cases and giving extra time to those
who needed a little more attention.

'How is it going?' Jane asked, when Emma took a break later in the morning and went into the coffee-lounge.

'OK, so far. I seem to have been prescribing antibiotics for nasty infections, and throat sprays and skin treatments for most of the morning.' She frowned. 'It looks as though a few of the visits I'm down for this afternoon are for a virus that's doing the rounds with the local children.'

'It's being cooped up together in warm classrooms that does it,' Jane acknowledged wryly. 'All those germs passing from one to the other with every cough and sneeze. I've just been doing my asthma clinic. The number of children on inhalers seems to be growing, especially at the local school. It backs onto fields, and you'd expect the children to be healthier with the countryfied atmosphere.'

'Depends what's growing in the fields, perhaps,' Emma commented, helping herself to coffee from the filter machine.

'I'm not sure. I can find out.'

'If it's anything that might cause problems for some children, it might be worth asking the farmer if he could avoid planting it next to the school for a year, then take a look at the results.'

Jane nodded, and reached for a notepad from her apron pocket. 'That sounds reasonable. I'll do some checking. Thanks.' She finished off her coffee. 'Time I was getting back to work. Talking of youngsters, by the way—I've arranged for a little boy to come and see you tomorrow. Oliver Hunt, a two-year-old. The health visitor thinks he might have an eye problem. I've put the details on file on the computer.'

'Thanks.' Emma put her own cup down on the tray.

'I must get on, too. My women's health clinic's waiting.'

Most of the consultations were routine, return visits for advice about smear test results and women coming in for HRT—hormone replacement therapy—checks. Her last patient of the morning, though, was Fran Halloway, a young married woman of about thirty, who had been referred to her by Jane after a Well-Woman check.

Emma glanced briefly through her notes, and said, 'Hello, Mrs Halloway. Please, sit down.' She could see that the woman was tense, and she smiled at her, trying to put her at ease. 'I understand from Nurse that you've been having a few problems. Would you like to tell me about them?'

'There's nothing specific that I can put my finger on,' Fran said uncomfortably. 'Just a general feeling of heaviness and discomfort, really. I thought it was PMT.'

Premenstrual tension could account for a bloated feeling, it was true, but Jane had mentioned other symptoms that she wasn't too happy about and Emma persevered, trying to solve the problem.

'Any trouble with your periods?' Emma asked.

'A discharge sometimes.' Fran pulled a face. 'The nurse said it might just be an infection of some kind.'

'Well, we'll know more about that when we get the results of the smear test,' Emma said. 'Perhaps I could examine you?'

When Mrs Halloway had undressed and lay on the couch, Emma asked, 'Do you have any children, Fran?'

Fran shook her head. 'Not yet. I wanted to get on with my career at the bank before I took time out to start a family. I want to think about it soon, though, in the next couple of years. Time goes on and you don't notice it, but I don't want to leave it too late.'

Emma examined her carefully, checking for swellings and any signs of discomfort. Fran winced a little under her gentle touch, which caused Emma some concern, and she said at last, 'OK, Fran. You can get dressed now and come and sit down.'

When Fran was seated once more, Emma said carefully, 'There does appear to be some swelling, but it isn't possible for me to feel it properly by examining you here, and I think the best thing would be to send you for an ultrasound scan so that we can see things more clearly. It may be that you have a small cyst which is interfering with your hormones and causing the discharge.' Fran looked tense, and she added quickly, 'They are quite common, so don't be anxious about it.'

'I've never had a scan,' Fran said. 'Will it hurt?'

'No, not at all,' Emma smiled reassuringly. 'Pregnant women have them without any problems. The only thing you might find uncomfortable is that you need to have a full bladder at the time so that the picture is as clear as possible.'

Fran groaned. 'I shall be bursting to go to the loo, I know it. I hope they don't make me wait too long!'

'With any luck it will all be over and done with fairly quickly,' Emma said, reaching for a hospital form and handing it to Fran. 'Take that along to Reception, and they'll arrange an appointment for you. Then you should come and see me for the results a couple of weeks after you've had the scan.'

'OK.'

Fran left the room, and Emma sat for a minute or two, quiet and thoughtful, fighting the sudden rush of memories that Fran's visit had brought. Charlotte's illness must have started in a similar fashion, not much in the way of symptoms but developing in an insidious, devastatingly unrelenting way.

She pulled in a few deep, slow breaths, then began to tidy her desk and gather the patients' cards, taking them with her to the office.

Still subdued, she scanned her list of appointments for the afternoon. There was nothing terribly urgent, and the thought of going back to the cottage for a short break was suddenly very appealing. She felt drained all at once, and she desperately needed to get away, to have some time to herself.

'Emma?' She looked up to see Daniel standing there, watching her closely, a frown around his eyes. 'Is something wrong?'

He had caught her off guard, coming in out of the blue like that, but she pulled herself together and shook her head.

'Nothing, I'm fine. I was just thinking of going home for an hour before my next stint, and grabbing a bite to eat. I could do with a change of scene.' She glanced down at her watch, then on a sudden afterthought asked, 'What are you doing back here? Is there any news of your father?'

'No dramatic change yet, but it's beginning to look as though they might operate in the next day or so if he remains stable. I came back to see how things were going here, and to make arrangements for my afternoon clinic. I wanted a chance to freshen up and get myself organised before I go back to the hospital, and there are a few things I shall need to collect from the house later.' He threw her a sideways glance. 'Maybe I could offer you a lift home? I didn't see your car outside. There isn't a problem with it, is there?'

'No, I left it behind and walked to work this morning,' Emma explained. 'There's a lot of sitting down in this job, and I like to grab the chance to exercise when I can.' She didn't think she was up to having company just at the moment, and added quickly, 'You needn't take me home. I'll be OK. I could do with some fresh air.'

'Did you want to take a shower as well?' he asked in an amused tone. 'It's raining buckets out there. Besides, if we go together you can fill me in on what's been happening here.'

She could hardly argue with that, and gave in with a modicum of grace. She had the feeling, anyway, that he wasn't a man who would easily take no for an answer. 'In that case, thanks, I think I will take you up on your offer. At least it will mean I have more time at the cottage.'

She reached for her jacket, slipped it on over her cream-coloured linen suit and went with him to the car park.

His car was solid and substantial, its paintwork gleaming despite the downpour. Inside, it was roomy and comfortable, and she sank back against the padded upholstery, letting the smooth purr of the engine soothe away the rough edges of her unhappy thoughts. She didn't much feel like talking, but she told him briefly about the morning surgery, and he threw in a question or two, listening to what she had to say, until he pulled up alongside her cottage and cut the engine.

The yellow stone walls were darkened by the rain and partially covered by the straggly remnants of ivy which curved around the front door and trailed beneath the windows. Emma looked at the scene and decided she must make an effort to get the garden under control before the winter.

Perhaps she was too quiet because Daniel sent her an oblique, thoughtful glance, and she wondered if she should ask him in. Her mood was still sombre after Fran's visit to the surgery and the bad memories it had evoked, but Daniel had been at the hospital for about twenty-four hours and had even more on his mind. Maybe he would be glad of the opportunity to talk.

'Would you like to come in and share some lunch with me?' she asked him. 'Nothing special, but I was thinking of soup and crusty rolls, and perhaps a salad.'

'I like the sound of that,' he said. 'Thanks.'

The rain had eased off during the course of their journey, and the sun was trying to filter through the clouds. She let them both into the house, taking him through the wide hallway and into the living room at the rear, where she dropped her bag onto a chair. The room overlooked a small patio, and she flung open the French doors to allow the damp fresh air in.

'The previous owners put the house up for sale and went to live down south. It was left empty for a while,' she explained, 'so I try to open it up whenever I can.'

'I can see why you were attracted to the place,' he said, looking around appreciatively. 'Big rooms, for a start, and that view—it's really something special.' His gaze went to the French doors and beyond, and scanned the fields in the distance, divided by lush, overgrown hedgerows, and dotted about with sheep. There was a white-painted farm house to the west on the rolling hillside, and in the east was the sprinkling of neat houses that made up the village.

'I'm decorating it, bit by bit,' she told him, 'but it all takes time. I started with the main bedroom, then went on to do the kitchen because that seems to be the hub of the place just now. I'll get around to the living room eventually, but it needs some thought to get it just how I want it. I think I may have to do something about the fire because the chimney-breast's looking a bit discoloured.'

Daniel frowned, looking at the darkened area she'd indicated. 'Have you been lighting it of an evening? It looks as though the flue might be blocked, and that could be dangerous. You ought to get it checked out.'

She grimaced. 'You're right, I suppose. I must get around to it. I haven't actually used it yet—in the short time I've been here I've been too busy to sit and relax. Mostly I've spent the time putting the house to rights and then collapsing into bed, but the evenings are starting to get a bit chilly now and there'll come a time when I'll need to use it.' She gave a quick, final look around, then said, 'Come on through to the kitchen. It's more cheerful in there. I'll put the kettle on.'

She had made the kitchen bright, with rose-patterned curtains, pine shelves and decorative crockery, and there were copper pans suspended from hooks on the freshly papered walls. In one corner of the room there was a pine table and carved chairs with plump cushions, and she waved a hand in their direction. 'Have a seat. I'll fix us something to eat.'

'I don't think I can just sit and watch you do all the work,' he said with a smile, moving over to the worktop. 'Let me help. I'm pretty sure I can toss a salad and lay the table without getting into difficulty.'

'OK, thanks. The salad stuff's in the fridge, and the crockery's mostly out on the shelves. You'll find the cutlery in the Welsh dresser.' She let him make himself useful, glad of the chance to keep herself busy, preparing the soup and setting the pan down on the hob.

Daniel managed to sort everything out and laid the table, and then said without preamble, 'You seemed upset back at the surgery. Was it something to do with a patient?'

She was still for a moment, biting her lip. She had been thinking about her sister when he had come along and disturbed her, and she had thought he had forgotten about that, dismissed it from his mind, but apparently he didn't give up so easily. He was waiting now, and after a few seconds she began to stir the soup and answered him carefully. 'There was nothing specific. My last patient of the morning had symptoms that might be due to an ovarian cyst, but I shan't know for sure until I have the results of some tests.'

'Are you worried about it? Do you think it might be more serious than that?'

Her shoulders hunched momentarily. She was concerned for Fran, but it was Charlotte's illness which had been uppermost in her mind. 'It's possible, but I've no way of knowing yet.' She served soup into dishes and carried them to the table. Daniel watched her, a small frown around his eyes.

'Why do I get the feeling there's more?'

'I've no idea.'

His eyes narrowed, and he said impatiently, 'If we're going to work together, don't you think we should at least try to be honest and open with each other?'

'I am being honest,' she said, more abruptly than she'd intended. 'I've told you everything of importance regarding the patients on my list, and there's really nothing else that you need to know.'

'About the patients, maybe,' he agreed. 'But I still

think you're troubled about something…you're keeping something back.'

His persistence unsettled her and she dropped the ladle down on the work surface with a faint clatter. 'It's really nothing that you need to be concerned about,' she said again. 'It's entirely my own problem and nothing whatever to do with work. I won't let it get in the way of doing my job properly, if that's what bothers you.' Jerkily, she went over to the kettle and poured boiling water into the teapot.

A groove worked its way into his brow as he watched her. 'It will bother me a great deal if you scald yourself because your emotions are getting the better of you,' he commented drily. He went over to her and curved his fingers around the handle of the kettle, carefully prising it out of her grasp and setting it down on the stand.

'I am not being emotional,' she muttered. 'You really don't need to keep a check on me. You can trust me to do my job competently, believe me.' Stiffly, she picked up the teapot and took it over to the table.

He leaned back against the worktop, studying the flash of her blue eyes and the upward jerk of her chin. 'I don't mean to give you the impression that you're under scrutiny. I sense that there's something bothering you, and I want to help. That's all. You're doing a demanding job, and it can take a toll of you even without problems outside work adding to your load.'

Emma sighed, and put down the teapot. 'I'm sorry. I know you mean well, but this is hard for me. It's personal. It isn't something that I find easy to talk about and, besides, you've a big enough load on your shoulders right now, without involving yourself in my problems.'

'Let me be the judge of that. I'm here to help, if I

can. Is this about your sister? You said she was ill, and you had to look after her. Didn't she recover?'

He was too perceptive by far. Her mouth trembled a fraction, and, swallowing hard, she moved away from the table and went to get bread from the sideboard.

He came over to her, and turned her to him, holding her still when she tried to resist, then tilted her chin so that she was obliged to look up at him. She fought to gain control of herself. She wouldn't break down in front of him. She mustn't.

'Tell me about it,' he murmured, his warmth and concern enveloping her.

She struggled to find the words. 'My sister died,' she said in a muffled voice, 'and I feel that I should have been able to do something... I should have been able to save her. I tried, but nothing worked... I felt so helpless, lost...'

'Was it cancer?' he queried softly, and she nodded unhappily.

'Ovarian cancer. We found out too late. She missed out on her health checks—she was too busy with one thing and another. Her marriage was on the rocks—'

She clamped her mouth closed momentarily, then went on, 'Steve left her... just walked out on her when she was pregnant, and she simply fell apart. She was so stressed out she cried for days, and made herself ill. She didn't eat, she wasn't sleeping. Then she had the worry of all the bills coming in and there wasn't enough money to pay them. If she hadn't been so unhappy, she wouldn't have neglected herself and she might have found the strength to fight the wretched disease. Instead, she put her symptoms down to stress and indigestion and PMT and did nothing about them until it was too late...'

'And you blame yourself for that?'

'I have to, don't I?' she muttered. 'I should have been there from the start. I should have known what was happening, but I was in another town and by the time I went to live with her it was already too late.'

'You're punishing yourself unnecessarily, surely? You don't have any reason to feel guilty. From what you've told me, you can't even have been fully qualified when this first started. Weren't you still doing your training?'

'Yes, but we kept in touch by phone, and we wrote to each other. Even so, I never sensed that anything was wrong.'

'How would you, if she didn't know herself? Besides, ovarian cancer doesn't usually affect young women— she was young, wasn't she?'

Emma nodded, and he grimaced. 'Then your sister was doubly unfortunate. You're still grieving for her, and that's why you're looking for reasons and laying blame.'

'I know, but I keep thinking that if things had been different…' Her voice shattered. 'I…'

Emma tried to turn away to hide the pain, but he stopped her, bringing her back to him and smoothing the wayward curls from her face in a gentle caress. 'Don't try to hide what you feel, Emma. You can talk to me, share it with me. Sometimes it's best to let it all out.'

His arms held her steady, drawing her into the solid comfort of his body, and warmth permeated through her, slowly taking some of the chill from all the cold, lonely places inside. 'What about your parents?' he murmured. 'Weren't they able to do anything to help?'

'They were killed in a motorway pile-up some years

ago,' she said thickly, her fingers curling tightly so that the nails dug into her palms. 'There was a bad fog, the road conditions were absolutely foul and another car swerved across their path.'

He let out a harsh breath, then said in a roughened voice, 'You must have been through hell.'

'I thought I was getting myself together,' she said slowly, 'but when Fran Halloway came to the surgery this morning it brought it all to the fore again…the difficulties of diagnosing something like ovarian cancer before it's too late to do anything about it.'

Daniel grimaced. 'That's where health screening comes in—making sure that women are aware of the need to go for their checks and talk about any problems they're experiencing. It's not all bleak. There are some promising diagnostic techniques on the horizon—looking for a certain protein, for one. Then there's transvaginal colour flow imaging, which looks at the blood flow of the ovary and shows up any obstructions.'

'I heard about it. And there's a procedure being used in the USA now—peritoneoscopy—which helps doctors to detect the stage of the cancer and allow sound treatment decisions to be made.' She sighed heavily. 'I keep thinking that if only Charley had gone to her doctor earlier, he might have been able to do more for her. As it was, she was too involved with the problems in her marriage, and then, later, she had to cope with Sophie on her own.'

'Sophie?'

'Her little girl. She's nearly four years old now.'

Daniel frowned. 'Who's looking after her?'

'Her father.'

He lifted a brow. 'He came back, then?'

'Yes. Eventually.' She didn't want to think about

Sophie and the way things were now. It stirred up too many inner conflicts that she couldn't resolve.

She drew herself up straight. She had to pull herself together and stop acting like a wet weekend. If she carried on like this, he would most definitely regret his decision to take her on.

'Your soup must be getting cold,' she said, making an effort to keep her voice even. 'We ought to finish lunch, and I have to get back to work.'

He looked at her closely. 'Don't you have any family at all, who could help you through this? Grandparents, aunts?'

'My grandparents are sweet, but they're quite elderly…a little deaf, and sometimes wobbly on their feet. They're very dear to me, but I don't feel I can burden them with any of this.'

'You need to find a way of coming to terms with what's happened, Emma. If you need to talk at any time, just remember I'm here. You won't do yourself any good by bottling it up, and you don't need to keep it to yourself. We're a team now, and I don't want you to be under any kind of strain.'

She forced a smile. 'Thanks. You've been very patient with me.'

His offer had been well meant, but he had also reminded her that they had to work together and, no matter what he said, she didn't think she could allow herself the indulgence of unburdening herself to him again. It wouldn't do. He was her boss, after all, and she didn't want him to think that she was impossibly weak.

He had his own problems, and he wouldn't thank her for swamping him with hers.

CHAPTER THREE

THERE was a nip in the air when Emma set off for surgery next morning, a little reminder that winter was not too far away. She was glad to get into Reception, where she found Alison, warming her hands around a cup of coffee.

'Mmm…that smells good. I hope there's some left.'

'Help yourself.' Alison smiled. 'I can't start the day until I've brewed up.'

'Me, too.' Emma poured herself a cup and went to look through the contents of her wire tray. 'There doesn't seem to be anything too urgent in here. I think I'll take my coffee through to my room and get organised. Everything's happened so quickly this last few days that I haven't had time to get acquainted with everything in there yet.'

'At least you know you're going to be settled now,' Alison said. 'Congratulations on landing the job. We're glad to have you here, you know. I thought you would be right for it when I saw you, and especially when you helped with Daniel's father. You looked so efficient and together.'

'Thanks. I must say I wasn't all that confident of the outcome myself.' Emma gave her a wry smile.

'It's understandable, maybe. There were several male candidates on the short-list, and perhaps he gave you a hard time. Women have caused him a few problems in the past, letting him down one way or another. His girl-friend had her mind set on marriage and planned on living in town where she could enjoy the status of being a doctor's wife, but I think he began to realise they didn't share the same outlook on life. He put her straight on a few things. All the same, I think it hurt when she took up with someone else and left for the city.'

She grimaced, and went on, 'That's all in the past, though. You'll do just fine here. We've moved things round a bit so the trainee will be using the room next to Daniel's when she comes back. It will work out better that way—we just never got around to sorting it out for her before. It was too convenient to use it as a storeroom for anything and everything, but we've had a clear-out since you arrived. It was well overdue.'

Emma smiled wryly. 'They've said that at nearly every place I've worked. It must be human nature to shove things away in the nearest hidey-hole. Anyway, I'm going to spend a few minutes making my room a bit more my own.'

She picked up her medical bag and cup, wedged the plant she'd brought in with her under her arm and went along the corridor to her room. Her own name plate had been fixed up on the door, and it gave her an odd little glow inside to see it there. Daniel certainly hadn't wasted any time arranging it, and somehow it made her feel more at home, as though she belonged.

She went in and set the plant down on a filing cabinet, then paused to drink her coffee, taking time to look around. Yesterday, she had brought in a low table and a brightly coloured crate of toys for one corner of the room. It helped to have them there for the times when she would be doing her child health clinic, and she had found that sometimes the play corner kept a youngster occupied when she might need to spend a few minutes talking to a parent. The only problem lay in trying to prise them away from it when it was time to go.

Now she took a few pottery animals from her bag and put them out on the shelves. Glancing around the room once more, she was satisfied that the place looked a bit more welcoming. About to close up her bag, she paused, then reached inside it and drew out the small, framed photo of Sophie.

The little girl was laughing up at the camera, her blonde curls tousled about her face. Looking at the photo, it brought a lump to Emma's throat. She ran her finger over the child's cheek.

Through all the heartbreaking time when Charlotte had been ill, Emma had done her best to fill Sophie's life with happier things, and there had been a lot of love and cuddles for all three of them to share. Now, though, both of the people she loved most in the world had gone from her life, and she sometimes felt empty inside.

'Is that your niece?'

The quietly voiced question made her jump, and she swivelled around to see Daniel, standing in the doorway. She had been so taken up with her thoughts that she hadn't heard him come into the room.

Her brief glance, before she looked away, left her with a strong image of his tall, powerfully masculine figure. He was wearing a dark suit which was immaculately tailored, and his shirt was crisp and fresh, the pale blue linen finely striped in a slightly darker shade.

She set the photo carefully down on the desk, and nodded. 'Yes, that's Sophie. She's a dear little thing, so full of life.' She dragged her thoughts away from the little girl. Lifting her gaze to him once more, she asked softly, 'How is your father? Have you heard anything more?'

'He's stable at the moment, and there's been some slight improvement. I'm going over to the hospital again later.' He looked again at the picture, and said with a frown, 'It must have been terrible for her, losing her mother. She's little more than a baby. How did she cope?'

Emma pressed her lips together briefly, then said, 'I don't think she quite realised what was happening. She knew that Charley was ill, of course, but she didn't really understand, although I tried to talk to her about what had happened and explain things as best I could. She accepts that her mummy was very poorly and is being looked after in heaven, but I sometimes wonder if she still expects to see her again one day. It's hard to get a child so young to understand that she never will, and I think that perhaps it's something that only time can resolve.'

She pulled in a shuddery breath, then straightened her shoulders. 'In the last few months she spent more time with me than with her mother because Charley needed to rest more and more, so in a way that might have made it easier for her. We were always close, Sophie and me.'

She didn't want to think about how Sophie had coped when Emma had had to leave. It was a question that still troubled her. The pain of separation hadn't eased much with time, and her only consolation was that perhaps Sophie, being young, had been more resilient.

'It might have been less traumatic for her if her parents had been in a more stable relationship from the outset,' Daniel murmured. 'Then her father could have supported her along the way. What went wrong with the marriage?'

'I think, basically, they married too young. They

weren't really right for each other, but Charley was vulnerable when they met. She was still trying to get over losing our parents, and I think she rushed into it without thinking things through properly. It just didn't work out for them.'

'You said that he came back?'

She nodded. 'Yes, he did, in the months before she died, but I don't think he could handle being around sickness too well.' Tension made her jaw stiff. 'After she had gone, though, he came back to live at the house. He wanted to make up for what had happened, and in the end he decided that it was time he took over the responsibility for Sophie.'

Daniel sat on the edge of the desk, watching her closely. 'That was a positive move at least, and I suppose it gave you the opportunity to get on with your own life.'

She pressed her teeth into her lower lip. That hadn't been her reaction. 'I would have carried on looking after Sophie, given the chance. I'd been with her for so long that she was like my own child, and it was a wrench to leave her.'

'But you got over it eventually?' It was a soft-voiced question.

She thought about it. 'I'm not sure that I did. I still find myself wishing she was with me.'

He said thoughtfully, 'Caring for a child, that is a big responsibility. You're young, you wouldn't have wanted to be tied down for long.'

Her chin lifted. 'You sound so sure of that, but you're wrong, you know. I didn't look on it as being tied down.'

'But you probably would have, given time,' he

pointed out reasonably. 'People are full of good intentions until other priorities get in the way.'

'I'm not other people,' she retorted dismissively, her
tone faintly challenging. 'There's nothing that would
get in the way of me taking care of her.'

'Except your career,' he tossed back, 'or your personal life.'

'Neither of those.'

The twist of his mouth derided her. 'You sound very
positive about that.'

'I am. Why shouldn't I be? There are always solu-
tions, if you look for them.'

'Which all sounds very good in theory, but it just
doesn't happen that way, does it? How many times do
you hear of children being taken into care because their
families can't cope, or children who take second place
to their parents' career ambitions? They all suffer in
some way, and I dare say few of them were damaged
intentionally.'

Emma flicked him a shrewd glance. 'You're a cynic,'
she said. She couldn't begin to explain the depth of her
feelings to him, and it would probably have been a
waste of time trying.

'Why didn't you stay with Sophie and her father, if
you were so keen to be with her? You were already
living there. Couldn't you have suggested it—acted as
housekeeper, or something? Or did he marry again?'

She frowned at that. 'No, he hasn't remarried. I did
stay for a time, but Steve wasn't really comfortable with
me being around. Perhaps I made him feel guilty in
some way because I had been so close to Charley.
Anyway, it didn't work out.' She pressed her lips together briefly, thinking about it.

'You're still angry with him.' It was a plain statement, straightforward, matter-of-fact.

She stared at him, fighting her inner demons. 'Angry? Why should I be angry?' She could hardly blame Steve because the marriage hadn't worked out, could she? But he had abandoned his wife and his child—that was always the thought that caused her pain. Her throat constricted.

'Because in part you hold him responsible for your sister's death,' Daniel persisted. 'Isn't that the truth?'

The breath left her lungs in a sudden rush, and she reached for the edge of the table, steadying herself. 'You're wrong, I don't blame him, not really. I don't blame anyone. It happened. Nothing will change that.'

She didn't want to think about it. It didn't do her any good to dwell on things, and the only way she'd been able to deal with the hurt was to keep busy. As she could now.

Restlessly, searching for something to do, she reached for a pile of medical books that she had brought into the surgery yesterday from home. Now seemed as good a time as any to arrange them on the bookshelves. Only, in her agitation, she had forgotten how heavy they were, and the stack began to slide, the uppermost ones beginning to tilt at a precarious angle.

'Here, let me give you a hand with those.' Daniel moved forward to take some from her, his hand brushing warmly against her fingers, his long, vibrantly male body gently nudging hers and sending a tingling shock wave of reaction coursing through her from head to toe. His nearness made her senses leap in a flash-fire acknowledgement.

She thought she heard his faint intake of breath, and her startled gaze tangled with his. He was very still, flame kindling in his grey glance, and when she swayed slightly his arm came up instinctively to steady her.

She needed his support. Suddenly, her legs felt strangely weak, and a pulse was beginning to hammer wildly in her throat. She swallowed, and made an effort to pull herself together. She wasn't sure what had happened, why her body had shifted out of control.

'Thanks,' she managed, her voice uneven. She looked down at the books. 'I'll just get these sorted out before surgery starts.'

He moved jerkily away from her. 'I'll leave you to it, then,' he muttered.

She watched him go, then leaned back against the table and waited for her heart to stop its crazy thrashing. Then, trembling a little, she started to arrange the books on the shelves.

When she was more composed, she rang the bell for her first patient. With any luck, the morning would progress uneventfully.

The little boy, Oliver Hunt, whom Jane had referred to her, clearly needed to be seen by an ophthalmologist. Straightforward examination showed her that one eye appeared to be turning inwards and would need correction.

Emma explained the situation carefully to his anxious mother, while Oliver played on the carpet in a corner of the room with a toy lorry from the box she had put there.

'He does appear to have a squint, Mrs Hunt, and I think the best thing to do would be to send him to see a specialist at the hospital.'

'Are you sure?' Mrs Hunt looked unhappy at the news. 'My friend was told that her baby might have a squint, but when she took her to the hospital they said nothing was wrong.'

'Well, appearances can be deceptive in babies,' Emma said carefully. 'The bridge of the nose tends to be more flattened in infancy, and this can sometimes make it look as though something is wrong. As the baby matures, the eyes look normal. In Oliver's case, though, I think we do need to do something to correct his vision.'

'He won't need an operation, will he?' Mrs Hunt asked worriedly, her fingers moving in a slight spasm of nervousness. She was a very slim woman, with sleek fair hair framing an oval-shaped face. She fidgeted with the strands, pushing them behind her ear as she spoke.

'Not necessarily,' Emma said. 'We hope to put things right without that, though sometimes an operation might be advisable eventually—when a child is older—but the surgery is generally quite successful. It only involves a short stay in hospital, and children usually get over the experience fairly quickly. But it may not come to that. We like to try a simpler approach first. Most likely the doctor will prescribe glasses to be worn for a time, with the normal eye covered by a patch.'

Mrs Hunt pulled a face. 'I don't like the idea of that at all.'

'It is an important part of the treatment,' Emma explained. 'By covering one eye, the child sees with the deviating eye and that way the normal connections between the eye and the brain are established. Without the treatment, those connections might be lost. The brain needs to assemble a three-dimensional image from the use of the two eyes together, and if it doesn't learn to do this by the time the child is six years old, then it's possible that he won't be able to see properly in his adult life. In Oliver's case, though, I think we should be able to deal with the problem and ensure that his vision is properly restored.'

'Lorry…brmm…' Oliver cut in, coming towards her with a toy, and she smiled at him.

'You've been very good,' she told him. 'I think you deserve a smily-face sticker.'

A few minutes later, Emma saw Mrs Hunt out of the room, and then went along to Reception to ask Alison to help the young woman to fill in a form for a hospital appointment.

'Bye,' Oliver said, waving a chubby little hand, and Emma waved back.

'Bye, Oliver.' His small, energetic figure reminded her of Sophie at that age, and she thought with a pang about the times she had spent with her lively little niece. She missed her so much…

Maybe she would phone Steve and take a drive over there. It was an early finishing day today as Daniel usually arranged cover for mid-week. The late afternoon was set aside for meetings so that they could deal with administrative matters, but there wouldn't be a meeting today, and it would be an ideal opportunity to go on a visit.

She looked back at the reception desk, and saw that Daniel was there, leafing through the post in his tray. He looked up as Emma approached him, and gave her a quick smile. 'All finished for the day?'

'All done,' she agreed, stretching her stiffening limbs. 'And you?'

He nodded. 'I'm going to the hospital to see my father as soon as I've cleared up here. Do you have plans for the rest of the afternoon?'

About to tell him she planned to go and see Sophie,

she hesitated, hearing a clatter as the main door was pushed open and a large man rushed in, carrying a young boy in his arms.

'Is there somebody who can look at the lad for me?' the man asked briskly, looking around him for somewhere to lay the boy down. 'He's been complaining of bad pains in his tummy. I think he should see somebody.'

'Bring him through here.' Daniel led the way to the treatment room and Emma quickly followed.

The man put the boy down carefully on the treatment couch, and the child, who Emma guessed was about eight years old, immediately doubled up in severe pain. She hurried over to him and stroked his hair lightly, trying to give him reassurance.

'It's all right, son,' Daniel said gently, noting his flushed and anxious features. 'We'll look after you. Can you tell me your name?'

The boy swallowed against the pain. 'James,' he answered slowly. 'James Colby.'

'Are you from around here, James?'

'Saxon Avenue.'

The nurse, Jane, shot off to see if she could find any notes, and Daniel turned to the man. 'Are you his father?'

He shook his head. 'I'm Martyn Hadleigh. I'm a teacher from the Coates Lodge School down the road from here. We've tried to contact the lad's parents, but he seemed to be getting worse and we didn't want to wait any longer. We thought we should bring him in.'

'OK. You did the right thing.'

Daniel turned back to the boy, who was showing signs of feeling nauseous and was nursing a kidney dish Jane had quickly given him.

'Let's see if we can find out what the trouble is, shall we, James? Have you been ill recently, any cough or cold?'

The boy shook his head, and Daniel carefully checked his ears, nose and throat, then ran the stethoscope over his chest. 'That seems to be OK. I know it's painful, James, but try to relax a little for me and show me where it hurts.'

James lay back and let Daniel examine him. He was very gentle, but thorough, and it soon became clear that the pain was mostly in the lower right side of his abdomen around the appendix, and had originated some hours earlier, with discomfort above and around the navel.

'So it was troubling you before school?' Daniel asked.

James nodded. 'Mum thought I was just making it up to get out of maths,' he said, wincing.

Daniel's mouth quirked. 'Not your favourite subject, I guess?'

James shook his head. 'But I wasn't really trying to get out of it. It really did hurt.' He was trying hard to be brave, but his lip quivered a little and Emma put an arm around him.

'We know it does. We'll help you to get better. Don't worry.'

'My mum isn't here, though, is she?' he said fretfully. 'She had to go to a meeting for work. She said she was going to visit some new people and it was important.'

Daniel frowned, and said comfortingly, 'We'll find her.'

'And my dad?'

'And your dad,' he promised. 'Just lie back and try not to get upset.'

He turned away from the boy to the teacher, and Emma noticed that he looked grim as he said in a low voice, 'Is there any news of them?'

'His father is at a site meeting, but we've left a message for when he returns. Our secretary's phoning the firm at regular intervals. His mother works as a buyer for a store in town, and she was *en route* to another place. We're still trying to get hold of her.'

Daniel acknowledged the information briefly and then gave his attention back to James.

'Well, James, it looks as though something inside you might be a bit inflamed and causing all the soreness you're feeling just now. I'll give you something to take the pain away, and then I think the best thing is to take you over to the hospital and let the doctors there have a look at you. When the hospital doctors have checked you over, they'll probably give you something to help you go to sleep. They need to see what's going on inside your tummy, and they might need to take the inflamed bit away so that you'll feel better. It's nothing to worry about, and you won't feel a thing, I promise. Are you OK with that?'

The boy looked at Emma, who smiled encouragingly at him, and after a moment he said, 'All right.' Anxiously, he added, 'Will you tell my mum and dad where I am?'

'Of course we will,' Emma said quickly. 'We'll get them to you just as soon as we can.'

Daniel drew up a syringe and injected James with a pain-killing drug, and after a few minutes the boy relaxed. After that he seemed to resign himself to what was going on. Jane stayed with him while Daniel and Emma spoke quietly together.

'I'll take him over to the hospital myself,' Daniel

said. 'He's getting feverish, and I think we need to get a move on in case the appendix perforates. I'd sooner not wait around for the ambulance, and I'm going over to the hospital anyway.'

'I'll come with you,' Emma said hurriedly. 'We can lay him down in the back of the car, and I'll sit by him to keep an eye on things.'

'OK,' Daniel agreed. 'Let's go.'

'Can I follow you?' Martyn Hadleigh put in. 'I think he'll be happier if I stay with him—a familiar face and so on.'

'Of course. While we're settling him in the car, perhaps you could ask our receptionist to let the school know what's happening and tell the head to send the parents directly to the hospital.' He turned to Emma. 'She had better talk to Accident and Emergency as well,' he added.

Within five minutes they were on their way, and Emma was thankful that Daniel's car held the road smoothly, with no jarring to their young patient. It was at least a half-hour journey to the hospital and the staff were waiting for them when they arrived. James was quickly transferred to a trolley and whisked off to be seen by the consultant.

'What happens now?' Martyn Hadleigh asked.

'They'll do a few tests to try to confirm the diagnosis of appendicitis, and then he'll need to be prepped for surgery,' Daniel told him.

'But what about the parents?'

'We should have their consent,' he said, 'and it would be a lot better for him if they were here to help him through it, but unfortunately they're not. If it becomes an emergency the surgeons will have to go ahead anyway.'

A nurse came through the swing doors and approached them.

'Mr Hadleigh?' She looked from one to the other and Martyn stepped forward. 'Do you want to go through and talk to him a while, just to reassure him?'

He nodded and went off with her, and Emma glanced up at Daniel. There was a tension about his mouth, and something else darkening his eyes.

'What's wrong?' she asked. 'Are you worried about James? I think we were just in time—we did the right thing, not waiting for the parents.'

'I know that. What kind of mother sends her child to school knowing that he's ill?'

'It might not have been like that. He said she thought he was trying to avoid school.'

'Surely she can tell whether he was making something up? Any parent worth their weight should care enough to find out,' he added tersely. 'And, besides, the way his illness escalated, he must have been ill from early on.'

'Do you know the family?'

'I know them well enough. I think she was more interested in her work and her meeting than in what was happening to her boy. It was too easy for her to dismiss him and go off.'

'It doesn't follow that she doesn't care about her son,' Emma said carefully. 'She might genuinely have thought he had a mild stomach upset that would pass, and if the meeting was very important—'

'Then she should have made provision for that kind of eventuality. It makes me angry when I see children being made to suffer because of their parents' thoughtlessness or lack of care.'

His annoyance simmered on. Of course he was concerned about the boy—so was she. But she sensed there was something else underlying his tense mood. Perhaps he was worried about his own family.

'There's not much more we can do but wait,' she murmured. 'Do you want to go and see your father? I can stay here and talk to the surgical team if you like.'

He shook his head. 'I'll go along there in a while. There won't have been any change in his condition to speak of or I would have been contacted.'

'Does he have any other visitors?' she asked.

'Mrs Harding's been to see him, and one or two of his friends. He's not responsive at the moment, of course.'

'What about your mother? You haven't said anything about her.' She was curious about the fact that she had never been mentioned in all this, and it occurred to her belatedly that perhaps he might have lost her and wouldn't want to be reminded of that right now.

'My mother is away in France, visiting relatives.'

'But you've tried to contact her?'

'No, I haven't yet. She and my father were divorced a long time ago, when I was a child, and she isn't a major part of our lives now.'

Was there an underlying bleakness in the words? 'But they must have loved each other at one time. Wouldn't she want to know what was happening?'

'Why should she? She has her own life, totally removed from ours.' There was an edge to his tone that Emma didn't understand, but it somehow matched the remote glitter in his eyes, and she realised it was a subject that still had the power to cut deep. 'The marriage broke down and she chose to go away, leaving my father to bring me up. She has her career, a wide circle of friends to keep her occupied. I doubt that she would want any reminders of her past life.'

Emma was shocked. It sounded so cold and remote, so alien to the way she thought about life and relationships. 'How old were you when she went away?' she asked.

'Around eight or nine when she made the final break.' He said it in a brisk, matter-of-fact tone, but Emma was chilled to the core by the knowledge. It horrified her to think about it. How could any woman bear to leave her child behind, and cut herself off from his life? How would a child of that tender age feel if his mother left him?

'Surely there was some contact between you afterwards? Visits, outings, birthdays?'

He shrugged. 'At first, maybe. But my father married again and we saw less of her after that. We get cards from time to time. The odd letter.'

Emma was having trouble taking it in. The picture he painted appalled her. She thought about how she'd felt, having to leave Sophie behind. It had torn her apart—and Sophie wasn't even hers. Yet she might have been, for all the love and need Emma felt welling up inside her.

She didn't voice any of those thoughts, though. Daniel might not understand, and she didn't want to risk having her shaky defensive structures demolished.

'I think I'll go and phone the surgery to see if there's any news of James's parents,' she said after a while. 'He'll perhaps feel a little better about things if I can tell him they're on their way.'

'I'll go and sit with him.'

He was frowning again, and she wished she knew why he was being so edgy. There had been coolness in his tone when he'd spoken about his mother, as though it still rankled that she had left, but surely, after all this time, he would have come to terms with his past?

Shrugging off her thoughts, Emma went and found a phone and called the surgery. Alison answered and told her that she had heard from the father in the last few minutes, and he was going to try to find his wife and bring her over to the hospital.

'That's a relief. James will feel happier once he sees them.'

'I expect he will, and Daniel, too,' Alison remarked. 'He was a bit uptight about the mother sending him to school, wasn't he? He gets angry at any hint of neglect or lack of care.'

'So I gathered, but that's rare, though, surely?'

'It is, but he tends to come down hard on anyone he thinks is out of order. His background's to blame for that, I suppose. It can't have been easy for him, with his mother leaving. It probably colours his judgement of others. Still, he does genuinely care about his patients.'

Emma rang off, thinking over what she had just heard. Alison had a tendency to let her tongue run away with her, but she had pinpointed something that had been puzzling her. Daniel was compassion itself with his patients, but sometimes she had glimpses of another side to him which was remote and untouchable, as though he had built a wall around himself, and perhaps now she could understand the reason for it.

She went back to the ward and found that the boy had been prepped for surgery. He was quiet, a little sleepy, and Emma stroked his hair and spoke to him reassuringly. She was overwhelmingly relieved when the door to the ward opened and a couple, who were obviously his parents, walked in. James's face broke into a tired smile, and Emma moved to one side to let the boy's mother come and take his hand in hers.

Daniel watched carefully as the woman kissed James's cheek and smoothed his forehead with her hand, and Emma wondered what he was thinking. She threw him a querying glance and gestured towards the door, and he went with her out into the corridor. He seemed more relaxed.

'I expect he'll be fine now,' he said. 'Why don't you go off home?'

'Are you staying?'

'Yes.' He glanced at his watch. 'I'm going to look in on my father, and I'll probably stick around for a few hours in case there's any change. You go.'

'I can give you a lift home, if you like,' Martyn Hadleigh offered, meeting up with them.

'Would you? Thanks.' She accepted gratefully, then glanced back at Daniel.

'Will you ring me—about James? Let me know if everything goes all right?'

'Of course.'

She went off with the teacher, and asked him to drop her off at the surgery so that she could pick up her own car. James's illness had made her decide to try and see Sophie. Then, when she was alone once more, she used her mobile phone to call Steve and find out if he was at home and ask whether she could go over there.

'Of course you can come over. Sophie will be glad to see you,' he said. 'She's been asking for you. ''When's Emmy coming?'' she keeps asking. ''Want to see Emmy.'''

Emma smiled at that. 'I'll be there in about an hour,' she said, and hurried to get ready for the journey.

*   *   *

Sophie came running to meet her as soon as the front door was opened. Her chubby little arms came up and Emma swung her up in a big hug and planted a kiss firmly on her cheek.

'Hello, sweetheart. I missed you.'

'Emmy—come in the garden. Daddy's making a bonfire. Come and see.'

They went through the house to the garden, and Emma was given a grand tour. The bonfire was made up of boxes and pieces of old wooden furniture, and assorted bits and pieces that crackled and spat and sent up showers of orange sparks.

'I've been having a clear-out,' Steve confessed, and Emma guessed it was more than just a bonfire. It was a ceremonial clearing out of all that was past.

Sophie thrust a stick into her hand and picked one up herself and together they poked at the twigs. Emma watched the little girl, seeing the intent expression on her face, and felt a surge of emotion well up inside her.

'Look, Emmy,' Sophie called excitedly. 'The paper's burning now. It's going all blue and crinkly.' There was a dark smudge on the soft curve of her cheek, and Emma had to resist the impulse to hug her all over again.

Later, when she sat in the little kitchen with Steve, sipping tea, she watched Sophie eating cake with relish. Her mouth was white with milk and covered in crumbs, and Emma smiled at her affectionately.

'Are you going to stay here?' Sophie asked innocently. 'Stay, Emmy, please, stay. Don't go away again.'

Emma shook her head sadly. 'I can't, sweetheart. Not today. I have to go to work in the morning, so I must go back. But I can stay and put you to bed tonight, and read you a story. And I'll come again to see you soon, I promise.'

Sophie looked crestfallen, and would have pleaded more, but Steve said briskly, 'You left your doll outside, Sophie. Go and bring her in—it's starting to rain.'

Her expression clouded, but without a word she did as she was told. Emma glanced at Steve, and saw that his own face was taut and shuttered.

'How's it going?' she asked.

'We get by,' he said. 'It's a lot harder than I imagined. She goes to nursery school during the day so I can go out to work, and somehow we muddle through the rest of the time. She misses her mother. She misses you.' He sighed heavily. 'Perhaps I'm not cut out to be a full-time father. I'm not sure I get it right, that I've got the right instincts—but I do want to make it work, just the two of us. She's my daughter and I was a stranger to her for such a long time. I owe it to her to be there for her.'

'You shouldn't be too hard on yourself,' Emma said quietly, remembering what Daniel had said about laying blame. 'Marriages break up. Things can't always be the way we intended, and at least you're doing what you can. You can always call on me, you know, to help out. I want to spend time with her and I'd like to have her stay over with me sometimes. It will give you a break, too.'

'Thanks,' he said shortly, and she wondered if his pride was getting in the way. 'I'll remember that.'

Sophie came back in from the garden then, clutching her doll, and Emma took a deep breath and said, 'You found her. That's good, we didn't want her to get wet. Has she had her tea yet?'

Sophie shook her head. 'I think she'd like some

cake,' she said and propped the doll up at the table while Emma cut another slice and laid it on Sophie's plate.

It was late when Emma finally left Sophie tucked up in bed and made her way back home. She hated having to leave her once again, and she felt an incredible weariness come over her, the bone-weary tiredness that comes on with emotional stress. All she wanted to do was to close her eyes and shut out the world.

It was cold in the house when she let herself in so she went into the living room and lit the fire, and let it warm the room while she made herself a hot drink. When she was ready, she went back in there and sat on the settee and switched on the TV to take her mind off things.

After a while, the TV programme seemed to drone on and began to fade into the background. The heat from the fire was making her drowsy, and she didn't have the energy to turn it down. Something at the back of her mind was struggling to come to the fore… Something she had forgotten? Something she ought to do? A vague warning echoing distantly?

But her limbs seemed to be weighted down, a dull lethargy was overcoming her, drugging her senses, and she gave in to the deep fatigue. She yawned tiredly, her eyelids becoming heavy, and gradually they drooped and she slid into a doze, and finally into a black, dreamless void. A draining, suffocating void.

Then later, much later, through the dark, inky cloud of sleep, something caused her to stir fitfully. A sound, a muffled noise.

'Emma?'

She was so tired. It was far too much of an effort to move. The darkness was peaceful, restful, and she drifted on a cloud of black velvet towards a welcoming cushion of oblivion.

'Emma.' More sharply this time. The sound was annoying, and she wanted to swat away the interference, but she couldn't quite find the strength to lift her hand. She moved restlessly. Something was covering her mouth and nose, and she tried ineffectually to evade it, her limbs sluggish, her mind leaden.

There was a breeze coming from somewhere, chilling her flesh and making her frown. Then she coughed and flickered awake briefly and tried to reach out through the fuzz of her brain to sort out where she was.

She made a feeble effort to sit up, but the attempt was too much for her, and she sank back down with a groan, feeling dizzy and nauseous.

'Come on, Emma. You've got to wake up.' Dimly, she recognised that gritty voice. She frowned. What on earth was Daniel doing here?

The thing, whatever it was, was still over her nose and mouth, irritating her, and she flapped at it again with her fingers. Once more the breeze wafted over her, and she shivered a little. Was she outside? What was happening?

Her eyelids fluttered open, and she stared foggily up into Daniel's slate-grey eyes. There were sharp diamond glints in the dark depths and she couldn't for the life of her think why he should be looking so tense and impatient, and something else besides. What had she done to make him look at her like that?

He tugged away the thing that had been covering her nose and mouth and she blinked up at him in drowsy bewilderment.

'Are we in the garden?' she muttered hoarsely. 'Where's Sophie? She was here a minute ago.' She frowned again, then moistened her dry lips with her tongue and tacked on, 'What are you doing here?'

'You're at the cottage,' he said, a thickened edge to his voice. 'What were you thinking of? How could you be so reckless?'

The cottage. Well, that made sense, at least. 'I live here…don't I?' As to the rest, she hadn't a clue what he was talking about, and decided it was too much trouble to work it out.

'I'm cold,' she mumbled. 'It's freezing in here.' She began to shiver violently, and he dragged her against his chest and pulled a duvet around her. She vaguely recognised the cover and forced herself to concentrate. It took her some time, but then she realised that she was lying on her bed. That was odd. She didn't remember coming to bed.

'How could you be such an idiot?' he growled. 'Didn't I tell you to get the fire checked?'

'I don't know what you're talking about,' she said heavily, her frustration mounting. 'Stop shouting at me.' She tried to swallow and found that her throat was like parchment. 'I'm thirsty.'

'I'll get you something to drink,' he said, and added, 'Stay there.'

She scowled. 'I wasn't planning on going anywhere,' she muttered.

He was being horrible to her, shaking her awake and then treating her as though she had done something stupid. What was he doing here, anyway?

Her glance went around the room. The window was open, letting in the chill night air, and that was where the cold breeze was coming from. There was an oxygen mask on the floor, which was peculiar, and she stared at it, dazedly wondering what on earth it was doing in her bedroom.

Then Daniel came back into the room and pressed a cold glass to her lips and she drank thirstily from it. It was milk, cold and refreshing, and she drained the glass, passing her tongue around her lips to clear the milky residue from them. She looked up at him, her blue eyes wide and a puzzled frown creasing her forehead.

'What happened? I don't remember coming to bed.'

'You didn't.' He retrieved the glass then sat down beside her on the bed and tugged the duvet more tightly around her. 'You put the fire on downstairs and fell asleep—remember? The fire must be faulty—didn't I tell you to get it checked?' He was sounding angry again, and she winced. 'The fumes filled the room, and you were being poisoned by them. I had to get you out of the room to revive you.'

'Oh.' She tried to absorb the information. 'But…what were you doing here?'

'I came from the hospital to tell you the latest news. You didn't answer my knocking at the door, but I knew you must be here because your car was outside and there was a light on in the house. I tried the door and let myself in.' He glowered at her. 'It's just as well that I did because I shudder to think what might have happened if I hadn't.'

She stared at him, a chill ripple snaking along her spine. Only now was she beginning to take in what he was saying, and the realisation of how close she had come to death came as a terrible shock to her system.

She started to tremble violently all over again, and with a muffled curse he put his arms around her and held her firmly so that she felt the warmth of his body slowly seep into her bones.

'It seems I can't let you out of my sight without you getting yourself into trouble,' he muttered.

'Not true,' she said earnestly. 'It's not true…really, I'm very competent…usually.' She looked up into his eyes, saw that the diamond glitter had turned to a brooding, smoke-laden grey that did nothing to soothe her jangled nerves. Was he still annoyed with her?

She swallowed. 'Thank you for what you did. Thanks for being here.' She moved cautiously in his embrace, tentatively reaching up a hand to touch his chest. 'It won't happen again… It's just that I was so tired…'

Daniel's mouth was firm and unsmiling, yet so very definitely male and compelling, and his strong-boned jaw was clenched as though he was holding himself in check. It was darkly shadowed, she noticed, and she felt an irresistible urge to trace the line of it with her fingers… Somehow, the thought became an action, and it was as though her touch triggered something off in him.

Slowly, his head lowered, and then, seconds later, his mouth touched hers and he was kissing her, a brief, hard kiss that made her senses whirl in stunned confusion.

Fierce sensation licked like flame through her body and left her reeling as though she were intoxicated. Perhaps she was, she thought wildly. Drunk with the feel of him.

Then, abruptly, he broke off the kiss, staring down at her, his breathing harsh. 'I shouldn't have done that,' he said thickly. 'I don't know what I was thinking of.' He frowned. 'You're not safe to be left alone.'

Emma shook her head, bemused by the flame that was still burning inside her, engulfing her thoughts and melting away her common sense. She missed his mouth on hers; she wanted the kiss to go on and on. 'I'll get someone to look at the fire…tomorrow. I won't touch it again until it's been fixed, I promise.'

His expression was deeply cynical. 'You said that before, and look what's happened. I don't have any faith in your promises. You can't stay here.'

'I'll be OK,' she protested. 'I forgot, but it won't happen again. I'll sort it out.'

'No,' he said briskly. 'I don't want to take any chances. It's too much of a risk for you to be here and, besides, it'll take some time to put right, and you'll have no heating while it's being dealt with. There's no alternative—you'll have to come and stay with me for a while.'

'I can't do that,' she muttered. 'Don't you understand? This is my home.' She felt constrained to make the point, but what was she afraid of? That she hardly knew him? That he was her boss? She blinked the thoughts away. Instinctively, she knew he was a man who could be trusted. He had saved her life. He was kind and responsible, and everyone who knew him thought well of him. Even so, she needed to fight for her independence, and she opened her mouth to protest again.

He got to his feet, silencing her with a look. 'Don't even think of arguing with me, Emma. You're pale and shocked and as weak as a kitten, and I've made up my mind. You're coming home with me now so that I can keep an eye on you, if only for a while, until you're feeling stronger. Just you stay there, while I go and get things organised.'

CHAPTER FOUR

DANIEL didn't give Emma time to think, let alone argue with him, even if she could have summoned the energy. Instead, he took charge, gathering together a few essential things that he decided she would need—clothes, her cosmetic case, medical bag—and then he stowed them all in the boot of his car. After that he settled her in the passenger seat, wrapping her up cosily in a travel rug. Within the hour she was installed at his house.

In the living room a log fire was burning cheerfully in the grate, and he guided her towards it.

'Sit there on the settee, while I go and make us a hot drink,' he ordered, and she did as she was told, too weary to fight him, sinking into the deep cushions and acknowledging to herself that she was bone tired. It had been a long, long day.

Waiting for him, she cast a desultory eye around the room, and saw that it had been furnished with care and an eye for comfort, with warm-looking upholstery and soft splashes of colour. She noticed there were flowers on the table and leafy plants feathering down on the wall unit, and masses of books arranged on shelves.

He came back into the room with a tray which he set down on a table by the settee.

'Here, drink this. It will make you feel better. You look all in.' He handed her a mug of hot chocolate and she accepted it gratefully, clasping her fingers around it and sipping carefully. 'Thanks,' she murmured. 'This is really good.' She stared at the fire. 'I hope I won't be in your way for too long,' she said. 'I'll get the repairs organised tomorrow.'

'There's no rush for you to go back to the cottage,' he said with a twist to his mouth. 'It'll be convenient, having you here. We're only two minutes away from the surgery so you can be on call at a moment's notice.'

She blinked, opening her mouth to say something about that, and caught the devilish glitter in his grey eyes and realised he was joking. She chuckled ruefully.

'You must be tired yourself,' she commented. 'You said you'd come from the hospital—is there any news?'

He was quiet for a moment. 'They operated on my father several hours ago.'

That startled her, but he had sounded withdrawn and she asked quickly, 'How did it go? Is he all right?'

'There were some problems…' His features were strained, she saw, and his usually mobile mouth was taut. He paused, then took a steadying breath. 'He suffered another bleed when they were trying to clip the aneurysm, and it was nerve-racking for a time.'

Her eyes widened, and she asked him, shocked, 'But he's holding his own now?'

He nodded. 'They seem satisfied that he's all right at the moment. The second bleed caused more damage, but it's too soon to say how it will affect him in the long term. If he remains stable over the next day or so, they'll remove him to the stroke unit for assessment.'

'At least he's getting the best care possible,' she said. The outcome was by no means certain, though. If his father came through all this, there could be some degree of paralysis, and whether that would be temporary or permanent was hard to say at this stage. 'They've one of the best stroke units hereabouts,' she reminded him. 'I'm sure if anyone can get him through this, they will.'

He nodded. 'I think so, too. I have to put my faith in them.' Slowly, he picked up his own mug and drank from it.

'You must have been worried sick,' she commented. 'And then to come and have to cope with me—it must have been the last straw.'

'Hardly.' His mouth quirked briefly. 'In the circumstances, I'm glad I decided to come away from the hospital when I did. There's nothing more I could have done there for the time being, and I know they're doing all they can for him. He needs rest now, and careful nursing.' He paused, then added, 'Young James came through his op all right, by the way. He'll probably be able to return home in a few days, and we'll take on his after-care.'

'I'm glad he's OK. Poor boy.' She looked at Daniel consideringly. 'After all you've been through, I'm amazed you found the time to go and check on him.'

'I didn't want to come away from the hospital, leaving loose ends behind me.' He glanced at her pale features. 'Come on, let's get you to bed. You're completely whacked out. I've kept you up too long, but I wanted to make sure you were fully recovered. There'll be time enough to talk some more in the morning.'

'I'm fine. You're the one who must need support.' He'd been through a lot and must have felt the need to talk. He had come straight over to the cottage, after all. She would have said more, but a yawn caught her unawares and she tried unsuccessfully to stifle it.

He gave her a lopsided grin. 'Upstairs, sleepyhead,' he ordered briskly. 'I've made up a bed for you in the spare room. Just let me know if you need anything.' His arm was around her waist, warm and strong and supportive, and she had to resist the urge to snuggle up against him. What was it about him that made her feel so safe, so secure, whenever he was around?

As it was, Emma slept deeply until morning, and it was only the sound of activity coming from downstairs that woke her. Clambering sluggishly out of bed, she drew back the curtains and gazed down at the garden. There was a wide sweep of lawn and a shrubbery and a rose garden, with a rustic seat to one side of a trellised arch.

It was a peaceful scene, and she would have loved to have gone down there and explored, except that a clock chimed somewhere in the house and she realised suddenly that she ought to get a move on if she was to be ready in time for surgery.

Quickly she washed and dressed, then hurried downstairs. A small pile of letters had landed on the mat in the hall, and she gathered them up and took them into the kitchen, where she heard Daniel clattering pans.

'I was just about to come and fetch you,' he said. He slid a fluffy mix of eggs onto plates which had been warming under the grill. 'There's tea in the pot and toast in the rack. Help yourself.'

'I didn't mean to sleep so late—I must have been dead to the world from the minute my head touched the pillow,' she confessed, placing his post on the table next to his cup.

'The rest has obviously done you some good,' he told her with a smile. 'You're looking refreshed and full of life. I can't say I'm used to that first thing in the morning.' His glance moved over her face, and slanted down over the cotton top and gently draped skirt she wore. He said nothing more, but something thoroughly male sparked in his eyes and her skin flushed with heat.

She sat down at the table and busied herself pouring

tea to hide her confusion. She sensed him moving about the room, and when she looked up again he was taking a seat opposite her and opening his post.

'From my grandparents,' he said, wafting a letter in the air. 'They're going to visit my father in hospital some time today.'

'Do you see much of them?'

'A fair amount. I try to get over to them at least once a week. They live on the far side of town, where my grandfather used to have his practice.'

'He was a doctor?'

Daniel nodded. 'And my grandmother was a pharmacist. I spent a lot of time with them when I was younger. They were very good to me, very loving and lovable. I was happy when I stayed with them.' He paused, and Emma thought about the small boy he had been and wondered how much they had tried to make up for the mother he had lost. It must have been a confusing and uncertain time for him then.

The phone rang, and he went to answer it, snagging a piece of toast between his teeth.

He jotted down some notes on a pad. 'Give me the address,' he said into the receiver. 'OK. I'll be with you in a few minutes. Try to get her temperature down in the meantime. Make sure she's not wearing too many garments, and you could try bathing her gently with a tepid flannel or sponge.'

He put down the phone. 'I shall have to go,' he said, gulping down the remains of his tea and hastily finishing off his breakfast. 'I hope this isn't a sign of how the rest of the day's going to be. It's a baby with convulsions, poor mite. Sounds like a virus of some sort. Will you be all right here, on your own? I'll see you later, possibly, at the surgery.'

'Of course. You go.'

Emma cleared up the breakfast things after he had gone, and then made a quick phone call to arrange for someone to come and look at her fire.

Surgery went smoothly on the whole. She dealt with aches and pains and sniffles, an abscess that would need dressing and a woman with abdominal pains that turned out to be the result of a bladder infection. She wrote out her final prescription of the morning and went along to Reception to give her notes to Alison.

Daniel arrived back from his visits while she was talking to Alison, in time to take a call from Mrs Jackson.

He was frowning as he put down the phone. 'Stewart's having a bad angina attack, from the sound of things. I'd better get over there. Mrs Jackson doesn't seem too good herself. She's an asthmatic, and she's not feeling all that well. She was having trouble getting her words out.'

Emma grimaced. 'It sounds as though you'll have your hands full,' she said. 'I could come with you if you like. I'm finished here until my clinic this afternoon, and I might be able to help.'

'Thanks.' He was already heading for the door and she grabbed her medical bag and went after him.

'Are you going to the hospital after this?' she asked as they walked to his car. So far he had fitted in visits whenever he had the opportunity.

'I thought I would. I might be able to at least spend an hour with my father. Want to come? You'll have time before your clinic, won't you? Unless you've other plans?'

'None at all. I'd love to go with you. I've been worrying about him all morning. Have you heard any more?'

She climbed into the passenger seat of his car and he started the engine. 'When I rang this morning they said he was awake and responsive, though it still hadn't been possible to assess the full extent of his problems. I expect they will examine him more fully this afternoon, and do what they can to set up a programme for his recovery.'

'That sounds encouraging, don't you think?'

'I do. It's more than I could have hoped for.'

They arrived at Stewart's house a short time later, and found him looking pale with shock and in a good deal of pain. Mrs Jackson was trying to help him but was breathing badly herself, and Emma could see that worry about her husband was making her condition worse.

'We'll look after your husband, Mrs Jackson,' she said soothingly. 'Try to relax, and I'll give you something to help with the breathing.'

Daniel took charge of Stewart, checking him over quickly and then drawing up an injection.

'This will relieve the pain,' he said, 'and I'll give you a sedative as well, to help you through it.' That done, he gave Stewart oxygen to relieve his breathing. 'Does that feel a little better?' he asked a minute or two later, and Stewart nodded briefly. 'Good,' Daniel murmured. 'Just take it easy. Relax. The worst's over. You're going to be OK.'

Emma could see that Daniel had things under control, and she concentrated her efforts on examining Mrs Jackson.

'It sounds as though you have a chest infection that's aggravated your asthma,' she said after a while. 'I'll give you a prescription for antibiotics. They should do the trick.' She helped Mrs Jackson to use the nebuliser that she had brought with her, and stayed at her side while she inhaled the drug that would relieve the spasm of her bronchial tubes.

Daniel was trying to make Stewart more comfortable, plumping up cushions behind him. 'I think you'll find you feel a lot better if you can sit up like this,' he told him. 'It'll take some of the strain off you.'

Stewart's features started to relax a little as the drugs began to take effect, and Emma guessed that the sedative was helping to relieve some of his anxiety.

'I've never had it this bad before,' he said breathlessly some time later. 'It seemed to go on longer and the pain was really bad.'

Daniel nodded in sympathy with him. 'Had you been doing anything strenuous before it came on?'

Stewart shook his head and Mrs Jackson, who also seemed to be feeling a little better now, said, 'That's what made it so worrying. Usually we can pinpoint it to his digging, or lifting things, or working too hard, but not this time.'

It probably meant that his angina was becoming unstable, Emma thought, and that meant he really needed to have treatment—most likely an operation to bypass the blocked blood vessels—as soon as it could be arranged.

'I think we really need to bring forward your hospital appointment,' Daniel remarked, echoing her thoughts. 'In the meantime, I'll write out a prescription for something to control the attacks, and you should go to bed and rest for a few days.'

'I can't do that,' Stewart objected. 'My wife isn't well herself. She can't spend time looking after me.'

'I can manage,' his wife objected.

'Is there anyone in your family who could help out?' Emma asked gently. 'Just to keep an eye on you both, and help with meals and so on? If not, we might be able to arrange some help for a week or so until you're both on your feet again.'

'Oh, I don't want strangers in,' Mrs Jackson said fretfully. 'I suppose I could phone Laura—our daughter. She might be able to pop in for a while each day. She works part time, but she would probably want to help out if she could.'

'I think that would be a good idea,' Emma said. She made a mental note to ask Alison back at the surgery to check on things to make sure the arrangements had been put in place. Otherwise they would need to provide back-up. 'Is there anyone who could collect your prescriptions for you this afternoon?'

'My neighbour, perhaps,' Mrs Jackson said, doubtfully.

Before they left, Emma had a word with the next-door neighbour, who had seen the doctors arrive and was anxious to help.

'I'll keep an eye on them for you,' the woman said. 'I'll go and have a chat with them in a minute. They've helped me out with lots of things so it's the least I can do. I've baked a cake this morning, and I'll pop round with some later and organise a meal for them. Don't you worry—and Laura's a good girl, she'll come over and do what she can. They just don't like asking for help, you know. They're independent souls, the pair of them.'

They left her to it, and Daniel started up the car once more. 'He seems OK for the time being at least, but he'll need angiography to find out which vessels are blocked. But my guess is he'll need a triple bypass.'

Emma agreed with him. 'The sooner the better, I imagine.'

Daniel didn't say much on the way to hospital, and Emma wondered if he was feeling anxious about his father. It was good news that he had come through the operation, but it sounded as though he would need a lot of rehabilitation, and that was bound to be worrying Daniel.

His grandparents were at the bedside when they arrived on the ward a while later, a tall man with a straight back and shoulders, and a fine-featured woman with a gentle smile. They greeted Daniel with welcoming hugs, and Emma thought of staying back, out of the way, feeling like an intruder.

She wasn't allowed to do that, though, because Daniel drew her forward and introduced her to them, and she was quickly made to feel that she was part of their small group.

'John's sleeping so it won't do any harm for him to have us all here, and the nurses are agreeable so long as we're quiet,' Daniel's grandmother said.

She was a fine-looking woman for her age, with a neat figure and clear blue eyes that met Emma's directly. Her face was gently wrinkled, softened by white hair that curled softly over her ears.

'So you're the new doctor Daniel was telling us about,' his grandfather said. 'It's good that he has someone to help him with the practice at last. Things have been difficult for him since his partner had to leave early because of the problems with her pregnancy.'

'Emma's been a godsend,' Daniel confirmed. 'I can't think how I would have managed without her.'

Emma smiled wryly. Hearing about his partner, it was no wonder to her now that he had had reservations about working with young women, and had wanted continuity. Still, he wasn't likely to suffer the same problems with her. She had almost forgotten what it was like to socialise, never mind get close enough to anyone to form a lasting relationship.

In the last few years, she'd had little opportunity for developing a private life. There had been her studies for one thing, and then Charley's illness had changed everything. She had put all her energy into taking care of her sister and Sophie, and though she may have dated occasionally none of the men she had been out with had made an impact on her.

She warmed to Daniel's grandparents straight away, though. They were united in concern for their son, who was resting peacefully, though he looked frail and ill.

'I'll go and fetch some hot drinks,' Daniel said, after a while, gently pushing her back down into her seat when she would have gone in his place. 'Stay and talk to my folks. I want to stretch my legs.'

She subsided, and turned her attention back to his family. 'This must have come as an awful shock to you,' she murmured.

They both nodded. 'Even more so for Daniel,' his grandfather said. 'He's always been specially close to his father. Only natural, really, with just the two of them for so long.'

'Didn't he live with his mother at all after the split?' Perhaps she oughtn't to be asking, but she was increasingly curious about Daniel's early years and, after all, his grandfather had brought the subject up.

He shook his head. 'It wasn't easy, because her work took her all over the place.' Emma looked at him questioningly, and he went on, 'Katherine worked as a journalist, first for a paper, then for TV. She never knew where she would be from one month to the next, so mostly his father brought him up. It was easier for Daniel to be with him and, anyway, he didn't get along with his mother back then. He still doesn't, come to that.' He paused, frowning, then went on, 'John simply took him with him to whatever hotel he was setting up at the time.'

Emma winced. 'Didn't he have a permanent base, a home to go to?'

His grandmother nodded. 'There was always the family home, though there was a lot of moving around in the beginning. When John married again they were relatively stable for a while, but it didn't work out and Ann left eventually. To be honest, I don't think John had ever really got over Katherine. It affected Daniel badly, of course, even though he never really took to his stepmother. Perhaps he didn't give her a chance. She was an outsider to him and maybe he expected it wouldn't last. He behaved abominably to her, almost as though he was testing her. Then, when she finally left, he felt that he had been proved right.'

So the bewildered child had been deserted a second time. First his mother, then his stepmother. Emma chewed her lip thoughtfully. Small wonder he gave her the impression he was reserved in his relations with women. It would be hard for anyone to get over that kind of trauma.

'Did he stay with you some of the time? He's very fond of you both.'

Mrs Maitland smiled. 'He came to us whenever we were free. We dealt with his moods, and patched him up and did what we could to make up for the way things were. It was very difficult back then, after his mother left. I don't think he ever really accepted it, and it's probably coloured his attitude to women and marriage even now.'

She pulled a face. 'He blamed himself at first. He was convinced he had done something wrong, and that was why his parents had broken up. Then he thought perhaps his father was to blame for sending his mother away, and that caused more problems. In the end, he worried that his father would leave him too, and after that he was just plain angry for a while.'

Perhaps he was still angry, deep down, Emma thought, still condemning his mother for her rejection of him, and too alienated from her to tell her that his father was ill. Yet his mother must care for her husband and son in some way, or why did she still send letters and cards?

Daniel came back at that moment with a tray loaded with coffee-pot, cups and biscuits, and she guessed he had charmed Sister into giving him the run of the kitchen. She smiled as she watched him with his family, seeing the easy affection that passed between them.

They all chatted quietly for a while, keeping an eye on John, who stirred briefly and made a few sounds which were mostly incomprehensible. Emma noticed that there was some paralysis of his face, and Daniel's grandmother gently wiped his mouth from time to time. He had been laid carefully on his side in a manner which would aid the rehabilitation of his weakened limbs, and after another half-hour or so a nurse came along and asked if they would mind leaving for a while.

'Go to Sister's office if you like,' she said. 'But I have to give him a rub-down now. We don't want him to get any sores.'

'We have to go, anyway,' Daniel said, getting to his feet. He turned to his grandparents and hugged them briefly. 'I'm still on call, and Emma has a clinic this afternoon. You two take care of yourselves. I'll drop by and see you one day soon.'

Emma walked with him back to the car, glancing thoughtfully at him as he climbed in behind the wheel.

'They are lovely people,' she said with a smile. 'I'm glad I had the chance to talk to them. Perhaps one day soon I'll be able to talk to your father.'

He nodded. 'Every day that passes is a bonus,' he murmured. 'I haven't dared think ahead till now. It's been one day at a time so far, but at least he's come through the first desperate hours and days.' He returned her smile fleetingly. 'My grandparents have taken to you. I'm sure my father will, too.'

A few minutes later, he dropped her off at the surgery and went to deal with another call that had just come in.

Emma worked through her clinic, then had a brief meeting back at the cottage with the man who had come to look at her fire. It was just long enough for him to condemn it, and point out a few other problems along the way, and then she had to head back to the surgery for the evening appointments.

Daniel was there, dealing with his own list of patients, and she stuck her head round his door between appointments to tell him the news.

'I may be with you for longer than I thought,' she said, grimacing. 'I have to have a new fire installed, but before they can do that they have to investigate a blockage in the chimney.'

His brows quirked upwards. 'Too many years of soot gathering?'

Emma shook her head, frowning. 'I can't say I understood it fully, but it sounds as though something was left there, which shouldn't have been, when the place was built. A lump of concrete, or some such, which is narrowing the passage and causing a backdraught, so there's a combination of factors to deal with. From the sound of it, it's going to be a messy business, and they'll have to make good the stone fireplace. I'll have no choice but to decorate when it's all done.'

'Good thing you hadn't already tackled it, then,' Daniel said. 'Don't worry about it. You can stay with me for as long as you like.'

'I don't want to get in your way,' she murmured.

'You won't. How can you even think that? I dare say we'll hardly rub shoulders—I don't seem to get a lot of free time at the moment, what with call-outs and the backlog of administration that needs to be dealt with.'

'Can I help?' she offered. 'There must be something I can do.'

'You're doing enough, taking turns with the calls. It's mainly the aftermath of Jenny leaving prematurely, and the work involved in having a student to supervise. She'll be back in a week or so, so I need to be organised. I'm simply glad to have you around.'

'Was Jenny having problems with the pregnancy?'

'Sickness, mainly, not just in the first few weeks. It never seemed to let up and it got so bad in the end that she decided she couldn't carry on here. She was planning on finishing anyway, because she wanted a year or so at home with the baby. It was just brought forward more abruptly than she'd intended.'

Footsteps sounded along the corridor as his next patient made an appearance, and Emma went back to her work.

*   *   *

The days that followed went by quickly. They were busy, and Emma didn't see much of Daniel because in the evenings he visited his father, and she was wary of intruding unless he specifically asked her to go along with him.

Fran Halloway came into the surgery one afternoon for the results of her ultrasound scan, and Emma told her, 'It looks as though you might have a cyst of some kind and we need to take a closer look at it. The consultant wants you to have a CT scan so that we can see it from all angles and decide what to do. How do you feel about that?'

Fran looked bemused. 'What's involved?'

'Nothing to worry about at all. You'll be given an outpatient appointment, and you'll be asked not to eat or drink anything for four hours on the day of the scan. Then you'll be given a special liquid to drink, which will show up in the X-rays. Once we have the results, we can think about the next stage.'

Fran nodded slowly. 'OK.' She pulled a face. 'I suppose if there's something there, it's best to have it looked at properly.'

Emma sorted out the forms that were needed, and went along with Fran to Reception to hand over the details to Alison. She looked around the waiting room, regularly full these days as the weather became colder and damper, and she was relieved that she had almost finished for the afternoon. It had been a long day, and she was looking forward to going home to Daniel's house and the log fire and the warm, cheerful kitchen. Daniel would be out again at the hospital so maybe she would have a relaxing bath and then make herself a snack and eat it in the comfort of the armchair while she watched TV.

At the house a couple of hours later, she piled her hair into a loose knot on top of her head, and then slid down into the bathtub and let the warm water wash silkily over her skin, slowly soothing away the day's stresses and strains. Iridescent bubbles released a gentle fragrance to tease her nostrils and she lay back and contentedly drifted a while.

When the water had cooled she stepped out of the bath and dried herself in a voluminous soft towel, then draped it around her, sarong-wise, while she debated what to wear. Something loose, floaty, to match her mood.

Stepping out on to the landing, she crossed the carpeted floor to her bedroom and walked straight into Daniel.

'Oh—' Her breath left her in a small gasp.

'Steady,' he murmured gruffly, his hands settling warmly on her bare arms. She registered his touch, and her skin heated in response. 'I didn't mean to knock you over. Are you all right?' His grey glance skimmed her flushed face and slid downwards over the creamy expanse of her throat and shoulders.

'Uh...yes...that is...I wasn't expecting you back just yet...'

'No... I guess not.' He laughed softly, his gaze shifting to the gentle swell of her breasts, captured by the knot of the towel. Amused appreciation flickered in his eyes. 'But I can't say I'm sorry.' His voice dropped to a husky murmur. 'You're beautiful, Emma. You take my breath away.'

His body was so close to hers, his breath gently warming her skin as his thumbs lightly brushed her shoulders, and for a wild instant she felt the urge to move into his embrace, to know what it would be like to be folded into his arms, have his hands stroke sensually over her body. He was long and lean and wonderfully sexy and she was finding it impossible to think clearly.

She wavered under the very male look he was giving her, and a pulse began to hammer frantically at the base of her throat. This was madness. What was she thinking of? They had been together five minutes and already she was fantasising about making love with him. How on earth would she face him when they had to work together if she gave in to that moment of insanity?

She drew back from him a little, and tried to get a grip on things. 'I thought you had gone to the hospital,' she managed. 'Did you change your mind?'

'Dad was tired so I left early.' He gave her a shrewd look, and reluctantly allowed her to ease away from him. 'I didn't mean to disturb you.'

'You didn't,' she lied. How could he help it? He was altogether too male for her not to be affected by him. 'I planned on making a toasted sandwich and eating it in front of the TV. Now that you're back, I'll fix something for both of us—if you haven't already eaten.'

He shook his head. 'Sounds good,' he said, moving away from her, but not before she had seen the reflective expression in his eyes, and she guessed that he knew she needed space.

Neither of them mentioned the incident again, and back at Woodhouse work went smoothly enough, and if they were both more aware of each other they were careful not to let it get in the way.

One evening, after surgery, Daniel went with her to the cottage to see how the workmen had been getting on. There was a lot of debris on the floor, though mercifully they had had the forethought to lay a plastic sheet over the carpet and drape the chairs with cloths. There was a layer of dust over everything, and it hung in the air and made her cough.

Gloomily, she stared around, and Daniel put a consoling arm around her shoulders. 'Try to imagine how it will look when it's all finished.' She absorbed the warmth of his touch and sternly quelled the fluttering that started up in her stomach. He was just offering comfort, nothing more. There was no reason for her heart to start racing.

'Do you think that day will ever come?' she said. 'So far they seem to deal with one problem, only to find another.'

'Of course it will,' he murmured, and she grimaced.

'I was hoping they would have it in place by now so that I could get on with the decorating. Looking at the mess, though, I don't think I can bring myself to tackle it.'

'I'll help you, if you like.'

'That's a wonderful offer.' She thought about it, then said, with a shake of her head, 'You've enough on your plate at the moment. Maybe I'll get someone in to do it for me.'

'You don't trust me to make a good job of it?' He grinned at her. 'Think what it will be like when your gleaming new fire has been installed and the stonework made good. You won't want to leave it then, you'll be so cosy in front of the coals. I'll have to come and prise you away to take surgery.'

She chuckled at the thought and he gave her a squeeze, turning her in his arms.

'That's better. We can't have you frazzled and upset. Scowling will put lines on that beautiful face, and that wouldn't do at all.'

Did he really think she was beautiful? She looked up at him in dazed wonder, a question in her eyes, her lips parting a fraction. His eyes darkened, and his hand lifted to brush the line of her jaw, his thumb lightly stroking the full curve of her mouth, making her whole body spark with anticipation.

'You've such a sweet, kissable mouth,' he murmured, and his head bent closer, and then his lips swept fleetingly over hers in a touch that was as light as thistledown, sending a tremor of excitement skidding along her nerve endings.

Daniel groaned, and tugged her to him, bruising her mouth with his own, teasing the softness of her lips with a kiss that rippled all the way down to her toes.

Her breasts were softly crushed against his chest, she could feel the warmth of his skin through his shirt, and her limbs were melting, a pool of heat growing in her abdomen as his powerful male body nudged hers, his thighs restlessly pressuring her own. Her pulses leapt as his hands explored the outline of her curves, easing her closer to him. His fingers were warm on the soft flare of her hips, and her blood streaked like wildfire through her veins, throbbing in her head until she was dizzy with sensation.

Emma gave a little moan in the back of her throat as their limbs tangled and her body clamoured for more, and through the haze of sensual excitement she registered that it was a good thing he was supporting her because she didn't think she would have stayed on her feet otherwise.

Perhaps he, too, needed a solid anchor, because he edged her back towards the wall, his mouth shifting momentarily to trail fiery kisses along the curve of her throat.

They moved together, and there was a rustle of plastic sheeting underfoot. Emma stepped backwards, her heel encountering a chunk of concrete that made her stumble.

'Oh— My foot…' she mumbled, fighting to regain her balance.

Daniel caught her, steadying her. 'Are you all right?' His voice sounded thick and rough around the edges.

She nodded, not sure whether that was the truth or not, her whole body reacting in confused awareness, as though she had been through some great upheaval. 'I'm OK. I'd forgotten where we were,' she said breathlessly, 'The mess, the rubble…'

He looked around the room, as though he were seeing it for the first time. 'So had I. Shall we get out of here? We'll go back to my place.' He took her hand in his and tugged gently, but she held back, slowly coming to her senses, fighting temptation.

Maybe it wasn't such a good idea to go anywhere with him right now. He was working on instinct, an urgent, male instinct that demanded satisfaction, and she sensed that things could get rapidly out of control. She didn't want that to happen, maybe because she was out of her depth, and she somehow knew that somewhere along the line she could end up getting hurt.

'What's wrong?' he queried softly.

She shook her head, not sure how to put her feelings into words. 'I think that was…a mistake,' she said huskily. 'I don't think it would be wise to let this go any further.'

He was very still for a while, then raked his fingers impatiently through his hair. 'Is that really how you feel? Funny, but I had the strong impression you were with me all the way back there.'

'I'm sorry…but that's how I feel.' She said it shakily, and turned away from him, moving to put a safe distance between them. She wasn't exactly sure what was making her cautious, but things could so easily go wrong between them and how would she deal with the chaos in the aftermath? Alison had said Daniel didn't have much faith in women, and she didn't want to give him any reason to lose faith in her. She'd been through enough upheaval for a lifetime…

She said jerkily, 'We have to work together… I don't want to spoil the way things are—'

'You didn't seem too bothered about that just a few minutes ago,' he said gruffly.

'Yes, well… I wasn't thinking at all. That was the trouble.' She pulled herself up straight, and looked around. 'We've finished here, haven't we? There's nothing more we can do to put the place to rights until they've finished clearing the blockage, and there's no point tackling the mess if they're going to make more. We may as well call it a day.'

He studied her thoughtfully, then said quietly, 'If that's what you want.'

She nodded, and they walked out to his car in strained silence.

CHAPTER FIVE

HAVING to work together, it meant at least that they needed to talk eventually, if only to consult over case notes, and the incident was pushed to one side by a kind of mutual consent. Emma tried to forget it had ever happened.

At Daniel's house, they shared meals and kept up a polite, if distant relationship, and on the evenings when they were both in together, they managed to keep busy with their own separate distractions, even if Emma did find it difficult to keep her mind from straying to him.

On Friday evening her phone rang when she was absently flicking through a magazine and Daniel was at the table, frowning over some paperwork he had brought back with him from the surgery.

She was surprised to hear Steve's voice on the other end of the line.

'Am I disturbing you, Emma? You're not in the middle of visiting patients or anything?' He sounded harassed.

'It's OK, Steve. Is anything wrong?'

'I just wondered if you could help me out this weekend—if you're not on duty, that is,' he added quickly. 'I have to go to London to find out about some work that's coming up, but my arrangements for taking care of Sophie have hit a snag. Is there any chance you could have her stay with you tomorrow and overnight? I won't be able to get back before Sunday because the interviews and discussions are taking place over the two days. I could bring her over to you.'

'Does this mean you're going to be on the move again?' He had worked in the oil exploration business some time back, and the news that he might be going away again came as a shock. What would happen to Sophie if he went? Would he take her with him?

'I don't know how things will work out just yet. It's all a bit vague right now. All I know is, I need to get my life under control and going back to what I used to do might be the answer.'

'But what about Sophie? What will you do about her?'

'I'll take care of her,' he put in quickly. 'I have to. I'm not very good at it—looking after a three-year-old isn't my forte—but I'm doing the best I can. I'll cross the rest of the bridges when I come to them.'

Emma absorbed what he said slowly. He was right. Taking one bridge at a time, that was as much as either of them could do for now, and he was simply asking if she could have Sophie stay for a while. She would leap at the chance to see her again, but how could she have her stay when the cottage was at sixes and sevens?

'I'd love to have Sophie stay with me,' she said. 'It seems like ages since we were together…but I'm not actually living at the cottage at the moment. I'm having some work done there, and the place is full of rubble and there's no heating.'

'Oh, I'm sorry. I didn't realise…' Steve muttered. 'I wouldn't have asked, only I really need to find out about this job. So far I've taken what's going, but I need to get fixed up with something more permanent.'

Emma struggled with the tremor of loneliness that crept along her spine. Just because he was looking for a job it didn't mean that he was thinking of leaving the country. It didn't necessarily mean that she would lose Sophie. She bit her lip.

'Perhaps I could work something out. The workmen may be further on than I thought.'

'Or you could come over here for the weekend,' Steve suggested.

'Yes, that might be a better idea,' Emma agreed. 'It would have to be after lunch, though, because I'm in the surgery in the morning. Would that give you time to keep your appointment?'

'Just about. Thanks, Em. You're a life-saver. I really appreciate this.'

'I'm glad to spend time with her. I'll see you both tomorrow.'

'She'll be ecstatic. She never stops talking about you.'

Emma smiled at that, and put the phone down thoughtfully. She would need to get organised, throw a few things into an overnight bag.

'Was that your brother-in-law?' Daniel looked up from his notes.

She nodded. 'I'm going over there tomorrow to look after Sophie.' She pulled a face. 'It might have been better if I could have had her to stay at the cottage— there are so many memories attached to her house. Whenever I go there now, I'm filled up with a mixture of regret and sadness… Still, it will be good to be with Sophie for a while.'

'She could stay here, if you prefer it.'

Emma's eyes widened. 'Here?' she echoed. 'But— You mean you wouldn't mind? I feel I'm asking too much of you already, just by being here.'

'I was the one who insisted you came here, remember?' He pushed his papers to one side with restless impatience. 'Anyway, why on earth should I mind? There's plenty of room.' He moved his shoulders, easing the stiffness in his muscles. 'It's a while since anyone's stayed in the guest room, mind you, but it shouldn't take much to get it ready. Besides,' he added, 'there's a bonfire display tomorrow evening on the Benton meadow. I should imagine Sophie would enjoy going to see it.'

His thoughtfulness made her spirits soar. 'Oh, Daniel, bless you for that. It will make the weekend much better if she can come here.' She made a quick smile. 'Do you know, I'd forgotten bonfire night was coming up?'

'Perhaps you should go and phone Steve, and let him know the new arrangement.'

'I will. Thanks.'

Sophie arrived with her precious belongings the next afternoon, most of the room in the bags taken up with her doll, a teddy bear and the pink comfort blanket that she took everywhere with her.

'Emmy, I'm going to sleep here,' she announced happily. 'I'm going to stay and I'm not going home for a long time, not till eleventy forty-three, tomorrow.'

Emma hugged her tight, laughing. 'That's a long time, isn't it, sweetheart? Lots of time for us to do things together.'

She introduced Daniel to the little girl, and Sophie stared at him solemnly. 'Is this your house?' she asked after a while, and Daniel nodded.

'We've got a room ready specially for you.'

Sophie shook her head. 'I'm going to sleep with Emmy,' she said bluntly, 'but you can have the other room, if you like.'

'Well, thank you,' Daniel said, suppressing a smile. 'Just as long as you're happy.'

'Yes, I am now,' Sophie told him. 'You can have Teddy to sleep with you, if you like. I've brought Dolly to stay with me.'

She thrust the teddy bear into his arms and Daniel accepted it with due honour, saying gently, 'Well, thank you, sweetheart. I shall sleep much better now, with him to keep me company.'

Sophie nodded, and tugged on Emma's hand, ready to explore the rest of the house. Emma threw Daniel a laughing glance and he smiled ruefully back and then followed them.

He drove them all to the bonfire that evening. Sophie chattered excitedly, and when they reached the field he lifted Sophie up, holding her easily in one arm, so that she could see when the bonfire was lit.

'There, can you see? They're lighting the bonfire now,' he told her, taking her closer to the rope barrier. 'That will warm us up, won't it?'

It was a cold night, and they had wrapped up against the weather in jeans and windcheaters and boots, and Sophie had dungarees on under her coat. Even so, Emma shivered a little when the wind stirred, and Daniel put his free arm around her and chafed her shoulders until the warmth seeped through and then he held her against him. It felt good, having him so close, his strength and support wrapped around her like a protective blanket.

They watched the fire hiss and crackle and shoot golden sparks into the air, then went over to the food tent to collect cheeseburgers and polystyrene cups of hot soup.

Daniel carefully handed Sophie her cup when the broth had cooled a little. 'Blow on it, like this,' he said, and then sipped carefully from his own cup. 'Mmm. Scrumptious.'

Tentatively, Sophie tested the steaming vegetables, and grinned back at him. 'Scrumptious,' she echoed.

Music started up outside, the sound of it swelling over the heads of the crowd through the loudspeakers set up at intervals around the field, and Daniel lifted her up again as they went out to see what was happening.

Sophie's eyes widened. They grew larger still when the fireworks were lit, and a thousand stars exploded in the black sky above them.

'Emmy, look,' she shouted. 'Look at the fireworks. There's a fountain, see, and a shooting star.' She watched it all in wonder and amazement, clinging to Daniel and banging him on the head with the flat of her hand to make him look too.

He grinned at Emma and hugged her to him. 'She's adorable,' he mouthed over the noise of the music and the display going on all around them.

'I think so too,' Emma grinned back at him.

They stayed to watch the last of the fireworks, and the glow of fire recede, and then, when the rest of the people started moving towards the gate, they followed. Sophie yawned widely and flopped around Daniel's neck, and he shifted her in his arms to make her more comfortable. Emma felt her insides grow warm, watching them together. He was so natural with her, so at ease.

Emma put her to bed as soon as they arrived back at the house, and looked down at the cherubic little face, peaceful in sleep, her golden curls spread out on the pillow. She slid the doll into bed beside her, and Sophie's arms went around it, snuggling it close.

Emma went back downstairs, and found Daniel in the kitchen, putting ground coffee into the filter machine and topping up the canister with water.

'She's well away,' she told him. 'I'd wondered if she might have trouble sleeping in a strange house, but she's out like a light.'

'All the excitement of the bonfire must have tired her out.'

He flicked the switch, and Emma said, 'Thanks for letting her stay here, and for taking us out tonight.' She reached out to lift the mugs off the stand at the same moment as he did, and his arm brushed the softness of her breast, his hard male body tangled with hers, and she registered the touch like an electric shock zinging through her nervous system.

Her gaze meshed with his. Heat smouldered in the depths of his grey eyes, and he said in a roughened voice, 'You don't need to thank me. I'm glad to oblige, but if you're going to carry on pressing that delicious body up against mine in that sexy way, you might well come to regret it. I'm glad you're pleased about things, but I'm warning you… I'm not made of stone.'

Dazedly, she said, 'I didn't mean… I just… I wanted…' She wasn't altogether sure what she wanted any more. She was distracted by the fact that he was so utterly, devastatingly male, and her body was signalling that she was aware of little else right now. 'I just wanted to say, thanks…'

'You did…beautifully…'

She became aware of his taut masculine response to her nearness, and her cheeks flamed, her heart pounding as though she had just run a mile. Yet she couldn't move, and with a muffled groan he bent his head and claimed her mouth fiercely with his own, kissing her with an urgency that made her heart judder, then frantically race, and when he broke off the kiss she stared at him, bemused, her pulses leaping, her whole body suffused with heat.

Then a noise disturbed the silence, a hissing, spurting, aggressive sound that started up behind them and brought her rapidly back to the present.

'The coffee…' His mouth made a straight line. 'Perhaps it's just as well,' he said on a resigned note. 'I should be keeping my distance. You don't want to get involved, and I understand that. You're probably wise not to tangle with me. I don't believe in love and happy endings, but that doesn't stop me from being a red-blooded male, with all my hormones intact and fighting fit.'

His hands flattened on her slender waist, then lifted her firmly away from him.

Slowly, his words sank in, and she backed unsteadily away from him. He didn't believe in love… Why was she shocked by that admission? Shouldn't she have guessed he would feel that way? And what was the matter with her, behaving in such a reckless way? What on earth had she been thinking of, letting it happen?

'I'd forgotten about the coffee…' she muttered raggedly, trying to pull her thoughts together.

From somewhere beyond the kitchen, there was another sound, a childish, long-drawn-out wail, and she stiffened instantly.

'Sophie…' she said huskily. 'Something must have disturbed her. I must go to her… I don't want her upset…'

Sophie was tearful, still half-asleep but sobbing fitfully and asking for her mother, and her cries wrung Emma's heart. 'Have you been dreaming, sweetheart? It's all right, now. I'm here, I'm with you.' What had brought the memories to the fore after their happy evening together? Perhaps it was just that the shared happiness had reminded her of other times, and she had woken in a strange house.

Emma sat down beside Sophie, and stroked her hair tenderly, comforting her as best she could, murmuring soothing words and telling her of some of the nice things they could do together tomorrow. After a while Sophie began to relax again. Emma stayed with her until she was sure that she had fallen into a deep sleep.

When she went downstairs again, she was subdued and thoughtful. Daniel handed her a mug of coffee, and asked quietly, 'All settled now?'

She nodded, and sipped at the hot drink. 'She was a bit disorientated. She has bad dreams sometimes.'

'And misses her mother. I heard her talking to you. Poor child. It will take time for her to get over it.'

'Yes, it will. I think she'll be all right for now, though. I tried to distract her by telling her we'll go to the park tomorrow and feed the ducks. She'll look forward to that.'

Daniel smiled briefly, but his expression was bleak, and Emma looked at his strained features and wondered if he was remembering his own childhood. How many times had he woken and called for his mother and realised she wasn't coming back? How many nights had he spent feeling lost and alone and abandoned?

But perhaps she had imagined that moment of vulnerability. He turned abruptly, and took his coffee into the living room, snatching up the evening paper on the way. Emma watched him abstractedly. He seemed totally in control of himself now, and why shouldn't he be? Life went on. Whatever had happened in the past was behind him now. He had simply grown a hard shell around his emotions.

Next morning, Sophie woke early and Emma gave her a hug and a big kiss. 'Hello, sweetheart. Shall we get you washed and dressed and see what we can find to do for the rest of today?'

Daniel put his head round the door as they were sharing a cuddle. 'Breakfast. Ten minutes.'

She helped Sophie to dress, and after breakfast, once the mist had cleared, they went off to the park as she had promised, armed with the remains of a loaf of bread to feed the ducks.

Sophie leaned over the rail as far as she could, with Emma holding on to her, to drop the crumbs to the scavenging creatures.

'They want some more,' she said, holding out her hand for bread. 'They're hungry.'

'I think they'll survive,' Emma said with a smile when the bag was empty. 'Let's go and find the aviary.'

Daniel lifted Sophie up on to his shoulders and they set off for the pet corner where the animal cages enclosed a grassed play area. Sophie looked, wide-eyed, at the animals, and then later ran excitedly about the playground, trying everything out.

Emma had packed a picnic lunch, and they sat at a bench table to eat it, thankful that the day had turned out dry and bright.

'Are there any more of those salad sandwiches?' Daniel asked, peering into the bag.

'Just egg and cress now, I think,' Emma said, 'or you could have some fruit. Here, help yourself.'

She pushed the bag towards him, and he would have reached in, except that Sophie pressed a half-eaten sandwich into his hand and said, 'You can have mine. I don't like salad much.'

Daniel surveyed the mangled offering. 'That's very kind of you,' he said, straight-faced, trying to suppress a smile. 'Are you sure you can't manage it?' He held it out to her, but Sophie shook her head.

'No. That's all right. You can eat it.'

'Thank you,' he murmured, and put it slowly to his mouth, as she watched him, while Emma started to chuckle and turned it into a cough. She half suspected that once Sophie's attention was distracted, the offering would go into his pocket.

It was some time later, after they had walked by the river for a while, that she said reluctantly, 'It's time we were heading back home, Sophie. Your daddy will be coming to fetch you soon.'

Sophie was engrossed in climbing a low stone wall, and said, 'But I want to stay, Emmy.'

'I know, sweetheart, but we have to go now, or Daddy will wonder where you are.'

'But I don't want to go back with Daddy, not yet, not now. Later. I want to stay with you.' Sophie's bottom lip jutted, and Emma felt a huge lump grow in her throat.

'You can stay another time,' she told her. Sophie was still reluctant, but Daniel scooped her up and gave her a piggyback, which took her mind off things, and after a while they set off back to Daniel's house.

Steve arrived about an hour later and stayed for tea and scones. He looked cheerful and refreshed, and Emma guessed that could be due to his short spell away from his responsibilities as much as anything to do with his future work prospects.

His handsome, square-jawed face was relaxed, and he shrugged off the jacket of his suit, laying it over the back of a chair. He sat down on the sofa next to Emma and stretched his long legs, thrusting them out in front of him.

'That's better,' he murmured. 'It feels good to loosen up after being in the car.'

'So, how did you get on this weekend?' Emma asked him.

He made a face. 'It's hard to say. There were a lot of men there who seemed really well qualified for the job. There was a lot of talk about the company's various undertakings, and sessions designed to introduce us to their management and find out how we all interacted. I shan't know anything for a while. They're still sifting through candidates and trying to analyse potential. I suppose they'll short-list eventually.'

Daniel asked him about the work, and oil exploration in general, and the two men talked for a few minutes before Emma found the chance to ask what was on her mind.

'If you do get the job, would it mean that you have to live abroad?'

'Most of the time, yes. But I would be able to come home every couple of months.'

'What will you do about Sophie? Will she go with you? It will take some getting used to, living in a strange country.'

He looked serious for a moment, then said lightly, 'We'll work something out. There'll be accommodation provided out there, and domestic help, but I'll cross that bridge if and when I come to it.'

Emma felt a sudden rush of panic surge in her at the thought of Sophie going away, but she managed to damp it down. As he had said, nothing had been decided yet. He hadn't even been offered the job.

Steve glanced over at his daughter, who was busy crayoning at the table, her small tongue pressed between her lips. 'How has she been?'

'Just fine. We've had a great time.'

'I'm glad. I knew she'd be OK with you.'

Sophie looked up from her drawing. 'This is me, Daddy, at the park.' She pointed to some bright squiggles next to a line of stalks. 'There's the ducks, see, behind the fence.'

'It's a lovely picture, Sophie. You'd better put your crayons away now, though, because we have to go home.'

'I don't want to go. I want to stay here, with Emmy.'

He shook his head. 'You can't stay here. Emma has to go to work.'

'I'll go with her to work. I want to stay here... please.'

Steve began to look exasperated. 'You know that isn't possible, Sophie. Clear up your things and get ready to go to the car.'

'No! I don't want to.' Sophie's expression turned mutinous, and she threw her crayon across the table. 'I'm not going.'

Seeing Steve's pursed lips, Emma thought it was time to intervene before things got out of hand. She didn't want to remember this weekend as one that ended in tears, so she set about calming Sophie and reminding her of all the things she had to look forward to at home.

'You'll be able to come and stay with me again, at my house. And you know that I'll come and see you soon, don't you?' she added on a positive note. 'Let's see if we can find room in your bag for your picture and the sparklers we had left over from the bonfire. Perhaps Daddy can light them for you when you get home.'

Sophie sniffed and rubbed her eyes. 'You can have the picture,' she said. 'I did it for you.'

'Thank you, sweetheart.' Emma clasped the picture to her, then put it in her pocket and patted it. 'I shall keep it near me until I see you again.' She smiled at Sophie and put her hand out to her. 'Shall we go and find your coat?'

'OK.'

Steve loaded her into the car, then said goodbye to Daniel and kissed Emma, giving her a quick hug. 'Thanks for helping me out.'

Emma kept up a bright manner until Steve had driven Sophie away, and her little waving hand had disappeared into the distance. Then, a little sadly, she went back into the house and started to busy herself, clearing away the cups and plates and stacking them up in the sink.

Daniel watched her turn on the taps and fill the bowl with foaming water and said, 'She went off happily enough in the end, but she obviously loves being with you.'

'But Steve is the one who has to take care of her now,' she said flatly. She rinsed the cups and transferred them to the drainer. 'I'm sure he'll cope as best he can.'

Daniel glanced at her thoughtfully. 'And, like he said, you have your work. It isn't as though she's your own child, and you can't afford to stand still and let your career pass you by.'

She nodded. What else could she do but carry on?

She didn't trust herself to air her feelings to him, though, and after a moment he said, 'I'm going over to the hospital. I'll see you later.'

Emma was on call the following morning, and her first visit was to see Tracy Walker, the five-year-old who had suffered from stomach pains.

'She's been like this since first thing this morning,' Mrs Walker said, showing Emma into the living room, where Tracy was doubled up in pain and screaming. 'I didn't know what to do, except to call you. She was sick half an hour ago.'

After a few initial attempts Emma could see that the child wasn't going to let her get close enough to examine her, so she concentrated on taking the heat out of the situation by talking to the mother in a relaxed way.

The sickness, apparently, might have been down to emotional stress, rather than any kind of virus infection, and could probably be discounted. The mother didn't think that Tracy had shown any sign of a temperature that morning, and there didn't appear to be any problems at school. She hadn't been sleeping too well, though, of late, and there had been a few nightmares.

Emma caught sight of a bonfire-night picture which had been Blu-tacked to a cupboard.

'Is this what she made at school? It looks as though she's been to a firework display.'

'She went to the one in Benton's field with her friend Hannah from next door,' her mother said. 'Hannah's parents thought it would be nice for her to go along.'

Tracy's sobs had abated a little, and Emma asked gently, 'Did you get near enough to the bonfire to see properly? I went as well, and there were a lot of people there.'

'We were at the front,' Tracy said, 'and my boots got all muddy when we went out of the gate.'

Emma smiled at that. 'It was a bit squelchy, wasn't it?'

By now Tracy was calm enough to lie on the settee, cradled across her mother's lap, and Emma managed to examine her, starting with her ears and throat, to belay any anxiety, and then gently checking her abdomen. It was soft, and there were no signs of anything that would need any further investigation.

'I think she may have had a touch of colicky pain,' Emma told the mother, 'but she seems to be feeling a bit better now. Make sure she drinks plenty of fluids, and if she has more pain give her a dose of the medicine to relieve the spasm. That should do the trick. Most likely, she probably just needs to be with you for a while to make her feel more comfortable and a little more secure.'

There could be a number of factors leading to the incidence of stomach pain and Emma resolved to have a word with Daniel back at the surgery about the family background.

Next on her list was young James, the boy who had had his appendix removed. The paediatric nurse had been visiting every day since his return home from hospital, and the sutures had been removed.

'I just need to check your tummy, James, to see if everything looks all right.' The operation site looked clean and was healing nicely, and she told his mother, 'That looks fine. He seems to be doing very well so I don't think he will need any more visits from the nurse. He should have another couple of weeks off school, and he shouldn't do anything too strenuous for a while. Let him rest as much as he wants, and make sure he has a nourishing diet.'

She smiled at James and said goodbye, adding to his mother as they went to the door, 'If you have any worries at all, let us know, but he certainly looks as though he's on the mend.'

At lunchtime Daniel went to visit his father again, but Emma managed to catch him before afternoon surgery. He was looking preoccupied.

'How is your father?'

'Frustrated, depressed. It's only to be expected, I suppose, given the extent of his problems. He's having physiotherapy, of course, but at the moment he's struggling to hold a hairbrush. The speech therapist is coming in every day as well to do what she can for him, but it's going to be a long process.'

'It's early days yet. Sometimes it's surprising how much progress can be made in the first few weeks and months. He's bound to be feeling wretched just now.'

He winced. 'I know. I just wish there was something more I could do.'

'Being there for him is what matters. He'll appreciate that, even if he can't show it.'

He nodded. 'I dare say.' He walked with her towards the office, where she was going to collect her list for the afternoon. 'How did your calls go this morning? Any problems?'

'No problems—except for a query about young Tracy Walker. She had another bout of tummy pain. Do you know the family very well? Might there be something in the background that I should know about?'

He frowned briefly, then said, 'The father and grandmother have been regular patients over the years. There are some nervous complaints—headaches, stress, sickness—nothing really tangible. I've not seen the father around lately, though, so it may be that he's working away. He's a carpenter–joiner as far as I recall, and does a lot of shopfitting work.'

There was nothing of great import there, but at least it added to the picture she was forming. She picked up her appointments list and scanned it.

'Looks like a busy afternoon ahead. Will I see you later at the house?'

'I don't know. I may not be back till late. I'm going straight from here to meet some of my father's hotel management team to go over a few problems with them. So far they are coping well, but I need to keep in touch so that I can put his mind at rest. Then I want to pick up some books on cassette tapes and take them over to the hospital. They might cheer him up and I'd like him to have them straight away.'

He went to get on with his own surgery and Emma tried not to be disappointed. He was being very thoughtful and professional with her, as she might have expected, but, perversely, she missed the close warmth they had shared before. Perhaps he was deliberately keeping a distance between them, or maybe he was simply worried about his father.

She suppressed a sigh and berated herself for being so weak and contradictory. Hadn't she said she thought they should preserve a professional working relationship? How could she complain when that was precisely what Daniel was trying to do?

She turned her thoughts to work. Somehow it seemed safer.

Fran Halloway was one of her afternoon patients, and she was anxious to know the result of her CT scan.

'We can see the cyst more clearly now,' Emma told her, 'but we need to find out more about the nature of it so that we can decide how to tackle it. It means that you need to have what we call a laparoscopy so that we can take a biopsy.'

Fran bit her lip. 'Does that mean you think it's something nasty?' Her voice dropped. 'Is it cancer?'

'The honest answer to that is that it's not likely, but we won't know for sure until we've had the results of the biopsy,' Emma said.

Fran held her breath, then expelled it slowly. 'What exactly is involved with this…laparoscopy?'

'You'll be given a general anaesthetic, and the surgeon will make a small incision in your abdomen so that he can look at the cyst through a thin, flexible microscope. It usually involves an overnight stay in hospital.'

'Will I have to wait long for the appointment?'

'No. I can get on to the hospital and arrange for you to be seen within a week or two. Are you agreeable to that?'

Fran's shoulders lifted. 'I suppose it's best that I know what's what,' she said. 'The sooner it's done with, the better.'

'Alison, our receptionist, will phone you and let you know a time and date,' Emma murmured, showing her out of the door. 'Don't worry, you won't have to wait long.'

Emma sat quietly for a while before she rang for her next patient. Every time she saw Fran she was reminded of Charley, and it seemed to her that life was simply not fair. So much could go wrong in people's lives, and all the professionals could do was patch them up and send them on their way. But maybe she was just feeling tired and despondent. Tomorrow she might look at things differently, and remember all the success stories.

She sent for her last patient an hour or so later, and glanced up to see Stewart Jackson enter the room.

'Hello, Stewart. How are you feeling?'

'Not so bad.' He chuckled. 'Better than last time I saw you, anyway.'

'I'm glad to hear it,' she said, smiling. 'I'll check you over, and then we'll sort out what's happening about your hospital visit.'

It appeared that things were reasonably stable for the moment, and Emma flicked through the notes on the computer screen to check the date he had been given for the angiography.

'Is somebody going with you to the hospital?'

'My son-in-law said he'd take me and the wife, and we'll phone him to let him know when I'm going to be sent home. How long am I likely to be there?'

'Your appointment's quite early in the morning, but you can probably expect to be there all day. You'll be given a sedative and a local anaesthetic, and you'll need to lie on an X-ray table for an hour or more while they look at the pictures to see what's happening in the arteries. After that, I imagine they'll ask you to stay on the ward for a few hours so that they can keep an eye on you after the anaesthetic and so on. You'll probably doze for a while, but your wife should think of taking her knitting or a book.' She smiled at him and he chuckled.

'Oh, she'll love that! Sitting knitting, and with me there, having to listen while she natters! Talk about a captive audience!'

She saw Stewart out a while later and then tidied up her desk. Daniel had already left by the time she set off for home, and she made up her mind to have a relaxing bath and then get something to eat. Perhaps Daniel would be hungry when he finally arrived home—unless he planned to eat at the hospital.

The phone went as she started on the evening meal, and she hurried to answer it, thinking it might be him.

'Oh…' said a woman's voice on the other end of the line. 'I was hoping to speak to Daniel. Is he there?'

'He's out at the moment, I'm afraid,' Emma said. 'Can I give him a message?'

There was a faint sigh of resignation that piqued Emma's curiosity. It sounded like an older woman's voice, but it wasn't likely to be a patient if she and Daniel were on first-name terms.

'It would have been better if I could have spoken to him, really. He always takes an age to get round to answering my letters, and I keep hoping that by talking to him—' She broke off. 'Oh, well, I suppose it can't be helped. Only it's his father's special anniversary— the day he opened his first hotel—and I thought I could send John a parcel to celebrate—or meet him to give it to him, which might be nicer. We met a while back and talked over old times, and we thought we might do it again. He isn't at his home, though… No one's answering the phone, and the housekeeper seems to be away so I'm not sure what to do now.'

Emma blinked, her mind switching a gear. It couldn't be…could it…? Was this Daniel's mother? She sounded so normal, and yet she had imagined…what? Some kind of ogre?

'Are you Mrs Maitland? Daniel's mother?' she asked.

'Yes, I am.' There was a pause. 'I don't think I recognise your voice, though.'

There was a question in the tone, and Emma said,

'I'm Emma Barnes. Dr Barnes. I work with Daniel. Look, you obviously don't know, but his father is ill and that's why you haven't been able to find him.'

'Ill? What's wrong with him? Is it serious?'

The woman sounded concerned, and Emma explained briefly what had happened.

Mrs Maitland was silent for a while, then she said, 'I must go and see him in the hospital. I'm still in France, though... I wonder if I could get an earlier flight... It will be too late now... Tomorrow...' She was thinking aloud, then she stopped and said quickly, 'Would you tell Daniel that I called? Tell him I'll ring back first thing in the morning? Will he be in then—about eight?'

'I should imagine so. He doesn't leave for surgery until about half past.'

Mrs Maitland rang off and Emma stared thoughtfully at the phone for a long time. She hadn't expected to feel any compassion for Daniel's mother, but she had sounded so warm, so genuine in her need to talk to Daniel, so anxious about her former husband. Then again, she had abandoned her child and that was heart-breaking, monstrous.

Or was there something more to the situation, some aspect that Daniel had blocked out? It mystified her, but there must be a key somewhere to unlock the whole sad truth.

The evening meal was cooked to a turn by now, and she decided that she ought to eat something now that she had gone to the trouble of making it. Daniel must have been delayed at the hospital, so she left the remainder of the casserole in the warm oven and tidied up the kitchen, her mind busily going over her conversation with Mrs Maitland.

When Daniel came in he looked bone-weary, and she

had to resist the urge to go over and put her arms around him. She wasn't altogether sure of the reaction she would get.

'You look tired,' she said. 'Has it been a long day?'

'You could say that.' He sank into a chair and leaned his head back, stretching his long legs out in front of him.

'Your father hasn't had a relapse?' she asked, concerned.

He closed his eyes. 'No. He seemed upset. He didn't want to listen to the tapes or look at the magazines.'

'I'm sorry.' She went over to him and put a hand on his shoulder. 'He might feel different about things in a day or so. Perhaps your mother will help to put him in a better mood.'

He threw her a narrowed glance. 'My mother? How did she come on the scene? I haven't talked to her.'

'No, but I have. She rang here earlier this evening and asked about your father, and said she would go and see him. She wanted to speak to you. I said you'd probably be in tomorrow morning if she rang then.'

'I don't want to talk to her.' His tone was clipped, his body tense.

'But she has a right to know what's going on, surely?' Emma was puzzled by his reaction. 'She wants to see him, and she was upset to find out that he's ill.'

'I don't want him upset and made worse by my mother turning up on the scene,' he muttered. 'His recovery is fragile at best, and he's already in a state of emotional upheaval after what he's been through.'

'Don't you think your father might look forward to seeing her? You can't know that he will be made worse—'

'But he might be, and I can't take that risk. This is

my family we're talking about, Emma. I'm his son, his flesh and blood, and I ought to know him better than anyone. I have to be the one to decide what's best for him.'

It was a dismissal of sorts, and she wondered whether she had really been guilty of overstepping the line and interfering in things that weren't her concern. Why couldn't he see that he was letting the feelings left over from the past override his judgement?

But he didn't want her help, he had made that clear enough, and that hurt. She stepped backwards, stumbling a little, and felt for the door.

'I'm sorry,' she said. 'I only meant to help. It obviously hasn't occurred to you that your father might take a different view of things. But you're right—it's your problem, and you must deal with it as you think fit.'

She hurried out of the room and heard him call her name, but she didn't pause and he didn't come after her. She went quickly up the stairs to her room and shut the door behind her.

Somehow she had to find a way to distance herself. Living together this way, it made her feel more involved in his situation, and it was all becoming too much of a strain to simply stand back and watch him struggle with the tensions of his family life. She was a natural, instinctive person, and it was hard for her to rein in her feelings and quell her impulse to speak out.

Perhaps she was getting too close to him for her own good. Maybe the best thing would be for her to move out, even if it meant going back to the cottage before the repairs were finished. At least it would give them both some breathing space.

Tomorrow she would ring up to find out whether it was feasible for her to go back there.

CHAPTER SIX

MRS MAITLAND phoned in the morning as she had said she would, but Daniel wasn't there to talk to her.

'He's out on a call, Mrs Maitland. I'm sorry,' Emma said. Given the way he'd reacted last night, it was perhaps just as well he was out. She'd wondered how he would have spoken to his mother anyway. His mood had been quietly brooding this morning, and Emma had kept out of his way.

The woman sighed. 'It can't be helped, I suppose. I wanted to ask him if there's anything John needs.'

'Perhaps you should try to reach him at the surgery.'

Mrs Maitland seemed to give it some thought. 'I don't want to annoy him by calling him at work. It's difficult enough to talk to him as it is. I'll have to leave it, I suppose. I was hoping I'd be back home before now, but I'm still at the airport. There's been a flight delay, but hopefully I'll be on way my home by this evening. How is John?'

Emma told her as much as she was able, and put the phone down a minute or so later. Mrs Maitland had sounded genuinely concerned, but would Daniel understand that? There wasn't much Emma could do about it at any rate. His manner had been withdrawn, and he seemed determined to keep his emotions locked away in a vault.

It was probably a good thing that Emma had a busy day ahead of her. At least surgery would take her mind off things for a while.

The waiting room was already filling up when she arrived at Woodhouse. The increasingly cold weather was taking its toll, and an outbreak of meningitis in the distant town had everyone on edge. Emma thought it had probably been contained, but that didn't stop mothers from worrying or coming along for reassurance. She went quickly to her room and rang for her first patient.

Halfway through her list, she was surprised to see Mrs Harding, the housekeeper, come into her room. There was a little girl with her of about three or four years, with silky brown hair neatly clasped with lady-bird slides. The child was well wrapped up against the cold, but she looked poorly and Emma suspected she might be feverish.

'What can I do for you, Mrs Harding?' she asked, as the woman sat down and lifted the child on to her lap.

'I hope you don't mind, but I wondered if you would have a look at Rachel for me? She isn't a patient here, but she's my granddaughter and she's staying with me for a while. My daughter has her hands full with the new baby, and I said I'd bring Rachel back home with me.'

Emma smiled. 'Of course I'll have a look at her for you. What seems to be the problem?'

'She's had a cough and a cold, and now she says her throat's sore. I think it hurts her to swallow and she's been off her food this last day or so.'

'Poor Rachel. It doesn't sound as though you've been feeling very well at all, does it?' Emma murmured, looking at the little girl's flushed features. 'Can I have a look in your eyes with this light? Good girl. That's fine. And your throat—can you open your mouth for me? That's lovely, Rachel.' She looked at the enlarged tonsils, reddened and covered with small white spots, and said, 'That is sore, isn't it? I think you have tonsillitis, chick. I'd better give you some medicine to help make you feel better, hadn't I?'

Rachel nodded, and Emma printed out a prescription.

'It looks like a bacterial infection,' she said to Mrs Harding, 'so I'm giving her an antibiotic to take three times a day. Try to make sure she takes it at regular intervals. In the meantime, you can give her Calpol to relieve the pain and bring her temperature down.' She handed over the prescription. 'Perhaps it's just as well she's not at home just now, with a new baby on the scene. We wouldn't want the baby to be ill as well, would we? What is it, a boy or girl?'

'A boy.' Mrs Harding smiled. 'The first boy. They've Rachel here, and Jennifer, who's eight. She's thrilled to bits with him and wanted to stay there. She'll be a proper little mother to him.'

'I expect she will,' Emma smiled. 'Is your daughter all right?'

'She's doing well now. There were a few problems on the way, and her stitches made her sore for a while, but everything's fine now. She's tired, though, and we—my husband and I—had to come back to check on the house, so I thought it would help if I brought Rachel with me for a few days. I was a bit worried by the sore throat, though. She's had a couple of bad throats in the last two years. Will it mean she needs to have her tonsils out?'

'I shouldn't think so. We often find that the attacks lessen as the child gets older so we generally like to follow a wait-and-see policy.'

She watched Mrs Harding and Rachel go out a few minutes later, and worked steadily through her list of patients until lunchtime.

Then she decided to ring the workmen at the cottage to find out how the work was progressing.

'There's just the finishing off bits to do around the fireplace,' the man told her. 'It's all set up and working, and the central heating should be back on line tomorrow. As to the rest, the painter finished yesterday and they're halfway through papering the wall. Shouldn't be too long now.'

She could live with the room half-decorated, Emma decided. At least the fire was working so she could heat the place up, and the debris would have been cleared away, presumably, or they wouldn't have started on the paintwork.

There was no real reason why she couldn't go back to the cottage today. It was just a matter of getting her things together and throwing them into the car.

Daniel's surgery was running later than usual that evening, and when he finally made an appearance in Reception he tossed the bundle of patients' notes into a wire tray. He carefully eased the muscles in his neck and shoulders, then glanced at his watch and pulled a face.

'I'm going straight over to the hospital,' he said. He glanced at Alison. 'Is there anything I should deal with before I leave?'

'I don't think so,' Alison answered. 'I'll just go and check for you.' She went over to the table to sift through her notes.

Emma said quietly, 'I hope your father's showing some signs of improvement.'

He nodded. 'So do I.'

She pulled in a deep breath. 'I shan't be at the house when you come home today. I'll move my things out this evening and go back to the cottage.'

'Even though the workmen haven't finished?'

'They're nearly there. Anyway, I've been away from home long enough.'

'You're running away,' he observed with a grimace. 'Why?'

She levelled him a steady glance. 'I need to get things back to normal, and I want to spend some time getting a room ready for Sophie so that she can stay over more often.'

'Do you think it's wise to get so involved with her?' She looked at him questioningly, and he went on, 'Shouldn't you be getting your life together, having children of your own instead of expending all your energy on someone else's child?'

'My life is together. She's part of it,' she answered him with a spark of defiance in her blue eyes. 'I don't need you to tell me what's best for me—what do you know about warm family feelings when you can't even talk properly to your own mother? How can you possibly advise me what to do? Sometimes I think you must have ice water running through your veins instead of blood.'

He raised an incredulous dark brow. 'Ice water? Ice? Are you serious? Whatever gave you that impression? Is it that I've tried to abide by your wishes and keep things between us on a professional footing?' His tone mocked her, his eyes glittering as he flashed her a look that was pure devilment. 'If this wasn't such a public place, my sweet girl, I'd like to show you just how fiercely ice can burn.'

Emma felt her cheeks heat, but she wasn't going to let that glinting look faze her. She bit back a slicing retort as Alison came over.

'Nothing for you, Daniel,' Alison said, skimming

through a wad of papers in her hand and oblivious to the tension sparking in the atmosphere, 'but there are some letters for you to sign, Emma. If you could do them now, we can just about make the last post.'

'All right. Let me see them.' Emma went with Alison to the desk, conscious of Daniel's gaze following her. Then she heard him turn and walk briskly to the door, and she felt a cool waft of air settle around her as he went out to the car park.

Professional, he'd said, and in her heart she knew that was how things had to stay. It was the only sensible way to go on. So why was she left feeling so utterly discontented?

Back at the cottage, later on, she was relieved to find that there was very little mess left behind to clear up. The newly repaired stone fireplace looked impressive, warmed by the copper cowl which overhung the grate. She lit the fire, and watched the golden flames curl around the nuggets of coal.

She looked around at the freshly painted room and the ceiling, which had been newly plastered with decorative swirls in pristine white. Two of the walls had been papered, and another was yet to be finished. She had decided to have it panelled, and she knew that it would look good when it was done, but somehow everything felt unreal, as though something was missing.

Perhaps she wanted Sophie to rampage through the rooms and bring the place to life. Or maybe it was just that Daniel's strange mood had left her oddly restless.

She went into the kitchen to make herself something to eat, and thought about going to soak in the bath for a while. Then she heard the doorbell ring.

'Steve?' She was startled to see her brother-in-law standing there. 'Come in. Are you all right? Isn't Sophie

with you?' She peered beyond him to the car, but there
was no sign of her.

'She's at a birthday party. I've to collect her in half
an hour or so,' he explained, following her into the living room. 'I was over this way and I thought I'd stop
by.'

'I'll make us some coffee,' Emma said. 'Make yourself comfortable.'

She went back into the kitchen and, instead of doing
as she had suggested, he came after her. 'I made a pizza
earlier,' she told him. 'Want some?' She retrieved it
from the fridge and pushed it under the grill.

'I wanted to thank you…for all you've done,' he said
awkwardly. 'I've never really said it before, but it
means a lot to me that you took care of Charlotte and
Sophie for all that time. I needed to let you know that
I do realise how much you had to sacrifice, with your
career and so on. I know I was wrong to leave them. I
was mixed up about everything then, and I let them
down. I can't make up for that, but I want to do my
best for Sophie now. I want to be there for her because
I wasn't before.'

'Charley and Sophie were more important to me than
my work,' Emma said quickly. 'I wanted to be with
them.' She set the food out on plates and sat down
opposite him.

He nodded. 'I know. But it still could have turned
out badly for you. Are things all right for you now? Are
you settled in this new job?'

'I think so.' She might have felt better about it if
things between her and Daniel hadn't been so unsettling
lately, but that wasn't something she could confide to
Steve.

She poured the coffee. 'How are you coping?' she asked, handing him a mug.

He gave a rueful smile. 'It isn't easy, being a one-parent family. I worry that I'm not doing the right thing by Sophie. This is all new to me. I want the best for her, but I'm not sure I always get it right.'

'How many people do? I think we all work on instinct, don't we?' She sipped at her drink, and added quietly, 'From what I've seen, you're doing a good job. Don't punish yourself. You can't change what's past, and Sophie's young enough to forget and move on.'

The doorbell sounded again, and she put down her mug and went to answer it.

She found Daniel standing outside. She stared at him, and saw that a flurry of snow had started up, leaving tiny white crystals glittering in his hair.

'Can I come in?' he asked, with a wry grin. 'Or do I have to stay on this side of the divide?'

His words prompted her out of her startled reaction and she pulled the door open wider, waving a hand towards the hall.

'I'm sorry. Come in. I don't know what I was thinking.'

He followed her through to the kitchen, where he stopped abruptly when he saw Steve standing there.

'Hello, there,' Steve acknowledged him, and received a brief nod in return. 'I'd better go, Em.' Steve rapidly swallowed the remains of his coffee. 'Sophie will be waiting with her goody-bag anytime now.' Then he hugged her firmly and turned to go.

Emma saw him out of the door, and went back to Daniel, who was standing in the middle of the kitchen, looking around at the scattering of mugs and plates on the table.

'I didn't mean to interrupt anything,' he said. 'I hope he didn't rush off on my account.'

'He didn't. He had to go and fetch Sophie from a party.' The kitchen seemed warmer, more homely, now that Daniel was here, but she quickly pushed away the fanciful thought. She motioned towards the coffee-pot. 'Help yourself. Is everything all right? You haven't had bad news at the hospital?'

He shook his head. 'No, I haven't. Things are much the same. They probably will be as long as Dad has no real motivation. Added to that, he still tires easily.'

'Have you tried taking in things from home that are familiar to him—photos, mementoes? There might be something that would give him a boost.'

'Yes, I've tried lots of things.' He gave a rueful grimace. 'Perhaps you were right, and it might do him good to see my mother.' His glance strayed restlessly about the room. 'I really came to see if you had settled in all right. I was in the area, anyway. After I came from the hospital I called in on Stewart—he had another nasty attack—and I wondered if the builders had fixed everything the way you wanted it, or whether you had any problems that needed to be sorted out.'

So he hadn't come especially to see her. Disappointment washed over her, and she made an effort to squash the feeling, asking, 'Is Stewart all right?'

'He's more comfortable now, but the sooner he has his operation, the better.' He looked at her enquiringly. 'So—has the work here been finished?'

'Mostly. Come and see.' She led him into the living room where the lamps burned softly, sending out golden pools of light, and the fire blazed warmly in the hearth.

'They've done a good job,' he said, looking around. 'You must be pleased.'

'I am.' She slanted him a brief glance. 'I'm glad I didn't have to put up with all the mess. Thanks for letting me stay with you while the work was done, and for having Sophie there as well. It must have been strange for you, having a child about the place.'

'It was fun, livened things up.' He frowned, adding, 'It made me think back to my own childhood, though, and made me wonder how things might have been. I don't have good memories of that time. Perhaps that was part of the reason for the way I reacted when you said my mother had called. It didn't help that I'd had a difficult day at work, and then there was my father's lack of progress.' His mouth moved wryly. 'It was just bad timing, I suppose. I didn't mean for you to move out before you were ready.'

Emma shrugged lightly. 'I feel more in control of my life here. It's better for me to be back on my own territory.' She studied his features. 'What you said this afternoon, about me having Sophie here…getting too involved… I don't look on it as you do. The way I see it, she's had a raw deal in life, and she's still so young. I want her to remember good times. I want to do what I can for her, to make things better.'

'But you risk losing out yourself that way. You're still young. You should be spending time with friends, making a life for yourself, instead of tying yourself down for the sake of a remembered bond with your sister. She's gone. That part of your life is over, finished, and Steve is the one who has to take care of Sophie now.'

'That doesn't mean I can't share in the process, does it? And it isn't as though I've cut myself off from the rest of the world. I still have a life outside work, and I just don't see any reason why she shouldn't be part of it.'

He made an impatient gesture. 'And how is Sophie going to feel when you do finally start to hanker for the bright lights and the night life? She'll suddenly find herself taking second place, you're not going to be around for her any more and her expectations will be pricked like a balloon.'

'Bright lights?' She flashed him a scornful look. 'You really don't know me very well, do you?' Her mouth firmed. His ex-girlfriend had a lot to answer for.

'I know about human nature,' he said, confirming her thoughts. 'I know that most people are full of good intentions but when they come face to face with reality they rapidly lose sight of them.' He flicked a glance at his watch, then said reluctantly, 'I have to go.'

'Can't you stay a while?'

He shook his head. 'It's getting on a bit, and I've some things I must do before morning. I just wanted to make sure you were settled in. I'm glad the workmen sorted everything out well for you.'

She saw him to the door, and watched him go.

When Emma arrived at Woodhouse next day, Daniel was busy in his office, taking a phone call from the trainee doctor who would be back on duty next week.

Emma glanced through her post, and saw that a date had been set for Stewart Jackson's bypass surgery. She asked Alison to contact him to come in for a chat about it, then went through to her own room to deal with her appointments.

It was a busy morning, and Fran Halloway was one of the first patients she saw.

'Do you have results of my laparoscopy?' she asked.

'They told me a few things at the hospital, but I'm a bit confused. They said I would need surgery.'

Emma nodded, checking through the hospital report. 'The report says that you have a cyst on your ovary which really needs to be removed, along with the ovary.'

'Isn't there any chance that it would go away on its own? I've been hearing about some cysts that simply disappear.'

'Some small ones do, that's perfectly true. But the type of cyst that you have could grow very large and might eventually obstruct some of your other organs, so it would be for the best if we could get rid of it.'

'It isn't malignant, though, is it?'

'No. But, again, this particular type of cyst could become malignant eventually, and that's another reason why you will be better off without it.'

Fran looked perplexed. 'But why do they need to take away the ovary as well? I was hoping to have a family eventually. I don't want to be catapulted into an early menopause. That's what happens if your ovaries are taken away, isn't it?'

'They wouldn't take away the ovary unless it was really necessary. It looks as though, in your case, the ovary has been damaged by the cyst, and it won't be possible to remove one without the other. That doesn't mean, though, that you won't be able to start a family,' Emma said soothingly. 'You will still have one ovary left, and that appears to be perfectly healthy. You would only have a premature menopause if both the ovaries were removed.'

They talked for a few minutes more, and then Fran left the room, still a little shocked by the recent news, but Emma thought that she was in a better frame of mind.

Emma's phone rang, and she answered it quickly, her thoughts still lingering on Fran's predicament.

'Emma? Am I ringing at a bad time? Your receptionist said I could have a quick word.'

'That's all right, Steve. I'm just between patients at the minute. What can I do for you?'

'I was hoping you might be able to help me out again. I've been short-listed, and the firm wants me to spend a few days at their head office. I wasn't sure what to do at first, and then I thought that if I could get Sophie into the nursery near you on a temporary basis, you might be able to cope in the evenings. I know it's a lot to ask, but I don't know anyone else that she'd be happy with. It's just for a few days. What do you think?'

Emma's mind whirled for a second or two. He'd been short-listed. Did this mean that in just a few weeks he would be on the move again, taking Sophie with him?

'Emma? Am I asking too much? I'm sorry. I thought of you first. Perhaps I ought to—'

'No…no, it's all right. I'll work something out,' she said quickly. 'What will you do if you get the job? About Sophie, I mean.'

'I haven't thought it all through yet. She'll go with me, of course, and I'll have to see what provision there is for children out there. It's early days anyway. I may not even get the job.'

But if he did? Emma thought about it. It would be like losing part of herself, to have Sophie move so far away… But Steve might not get the job after all. He might find work here, close to home, so worrying now was pointless. In the meantime, she would spend what time she could with Sophie. 'If you can sort it out with the local nursery…'

If Sophie could settle at the nursery, it might be feasible to have her stay overnight, but she would need to arrange cover for when the nursery was closed if she was on duty. Maybe the health visitor would know of someone reliable and motherly who could cover for the in-between times.

'Bless you, Em. I'll sort out all the arrangements and get back to you.'

It was an effort to drag her mind back to the work in hand after he had rung off. Inside, she was sad, thinking about what she would do if Sophie went away. Maybe she would be able to go and visit sometimes.

Eventually, the number of patients waiting to be seen dwindled to none, and she switched off the computer and went along to Reception.

Mrs Harding was there, with Rachel, and Emma stopped to say hello.

'You're looking more cheerful, Rachel,' she greeted her. 'Is your throat all right now?'

'Yes. It's all better now,' the little girl said. 'I still can't eat swedes, though,' she added, looking up at her grandmother as if expecting an argument.

Emma and Mrs Harding laughed. 'There, and I thought the medicine would work wonders,' Mrs Harding said. 'I'm just waiting to see if I could get an appointment with the nurse,' she confided. 'I've had a cold this last week, like Rachel here, and I think it's caused a bit of a problem with my ears. I tried to ignore it, but it's not going away.'

'I'll take a look for you, if you like,' Emma said. 'Come into the surgery, and we'll see if we can find out what the problem is.'

'Would you? I didn't like to ask. I know you are all very busy.'

The ear turned out to be inflamed, and Emma prescribed some drops to clear it up.

'Thanks very much,' Mrs Harding said. 'I don't like to keep bothering you like this, but it's been one thing after another lately.'

'That's all right. Don't you worry about it.' A sudden thought struck Emma, and she added hurriedly, 'I wonder if you could help me out with something, Mrs Harding?'

'Call me Sandra, love. What can I do for you?'

Emma outlined the problem of Sophie coming over and the out-of-hours care she might need. 'It's just a question of collecting her from the nursery if I'm working late here, or out on call,' she explained. 'Do you know anyone hereabouts who would be able to do it for me? Someone sensible and trustworthy?'

'Well, there's always me, of course,' Sandra said brightly. 'I'll have Rachel with me until the middle of next week, so they'd be good playmates for each other, I should think. Don't give it another thought. Just give me a ring, whenever.'

Emma was cheered by the offer. She gave the woman a hug. 'Thanks, Sandra. That's wonderful.'

When Sophie came to stay, she brought the first real snow of the season with her. It covered everything with a fine white blanket, and Sophie delighted in making tracks in it with her boots.

'We'll make a snowman, shall we?' Emma suggested, 'before the sun comes and melts it all away?'

They were engrossed in the task, hunting around for pebbles for the eyes and nose, when a car pulled up in the road alongside the cottage. Emma glanced up a moment or so later to see Daniel standing in the drive, watching them with an odd expression on his face. He was dressed in jeans and a windcheater, and he looked tall and strong and bone-meltingly, powerfully male.

'We need buttons for his coat,' Sophie called to him.

Emma's mouth tilted at the corners. 'I think that means you have to help us find them,' she said, still taking in his presence and giving herself time to calm down and slow the erratic beat of her pulse.

He sent her a crooked grin, and began a search of the path where the snow was showing signs of melting away.

'Are you sure he'll last long enough to get them in place?' he murmured, casting a weather eye at the sky.

Emma tossed a snowball at his jacket, catching him squarely on the chest, and a scramble followed, with balls of snow flying in all directions. Sophie thought it was great fun, and her shouts of delight filled the air until Emma scooped her up and bundled her inside.

'Come on. We'd better get you warm and dry. We'll have hot chocolate and marshmallows,' she said. 'How does that sound?'

'Mmm-mmm,' Sophie said, stamping her boots on the mat. 'That sounds scrummy-yummy.'

Daniel helped her off with her coat and boots while Emma busied herself at the hob.

'I didn't realise you would have Sophie with you today,' he said, when Sophie had scrambled off to put her doll in its pram. 'Is she staying over?'

'Just for a few days,' Emma murmured, pouring milk into the mugs and stirring the hot chocolate. 'I haven't seen you to talk to you for a while,' she admitted.

'You've been so busy lately. Is your father making any progress?'

'Things are looking up. He was able to do more things for himself when I saw him this morning, and the physios are working on his sense of balance. His concentration's improving as well.'

'Oh, that's wonderful. I'm so glad for you—for him. What happened to bring about the change, do you know?'

Sophie clattered back into the room with her doll's pram, distracting her, but when she looked up she saw that Daniel's smile was slightly awry.

'I suspect it was something to do with my mother. I can't think of any other explanation for it.'

Emma's brow lifted. 'Has she been to see him?'

'Yes. I sounded him out about how he would feel if she was to visit, and he seemed to like the idea.'

'You were wary before, though.'

'He's always been touchy about her. Half the time I thought his blood pressure would start to rise just at the mention of her name.'

'A lot like yours, then?' she murmured cheekily.

His mouth twitched at her retort, but he didn't have time to answer because Sophie thrust her doll into his arms.

'Baby wants a drink as well,' she told him. 'Have you got a cup for her?'

'I expect we can find one,' Daniel said with a smile. 'Let's have a look, shall we?'

Emma watched him with the little girl, and thought how gentle he was, how carefully he listened to what she had to say. It was just the same at Woodhouse, or when he was on call. Whenever she had seen him with children he had shown the same instinctive understanding, the same depth of care.

It was good to see him looking relaxed, and that had to be because his father was on the mend. She was glad for him.

He stayed with them for another hour or so, then reluctantly prepared to leave.

'Aren't you going to stay and have lunch with us?' Emma asked.

'I can't. I promised I'd go and visit my grandparents.'

Sophie looked crestfallen, and he said gently, 'You'll still be here tomorrow, won't you?' She nodded and he gave her a cuddle. 'That's all right, then. Perhaps we could all go to the fair in the evening if Emma doesn't have anything else planned?'

Emma shook her head, her spirits rising like mercury at the thought of seeing him again. 'That sounds like a brilliant idea.'

'Good. That's settled, then. I'll come and pick you both up after work.'

He went out to his car, pulling the collar of his coat up against the cold, and Emma stood with Sophie and watched him go, looking at the way his hair lay crisply at the back of his head and wishing she could run her hands through it and feel its springiness. She had missed being with him, felt miserable when he wasn't close by, and now she was feeling a surge of joy because he had sought her out.

But there was a tinge of danger mixed with the pleasure. Dared she risk getting emotionally tangled with a man whose attitude to love was skewed because of his traumatic past? Her mouth twisted. Wasn't it too late to be asking herself that?

Stewart Jackson came into the surgery next day for a repeat of his prescription and reassurance in general.

'Can you tell me something more about this operation Doc Maitland says I need? How will they get round the blocked arteries?' he asked. 'Is it going to make much difference to the way I am now?'

'It should make a lot of difference,' Emma told him. 'They'll probably need to graft some tissue from a blood vessel in your leg to bypass the narrowed arteries. Once that's done, your circulation should improve and you'll find you get relief from the angina pain.'

'Will it take long before I'm back on my feet?'

'It'll probably take you a few weeks to recover fully from the surgery and get fit again. Of course, you'll need to keep to a sensible diet to keep your cholesterol down, and definitely no smoking.' She talked to him for a little longer, and he seemed more at ease when he eventually left.

It was getting on for lunchtime when she saw the last of her patients out of the surgery, and she went over to the nursery to collect Sophie for a couple of hours. They shared a meal and Emma listened to Sophie's excited chatter about the morning's activities until it was time to go back to Woodhouse to deal with the afternoon appointments.

It all went smoothly enough, and she was glad to keep busy. It kept her mind from wandering to Daniel and the evening ahead.

She and Sophie were ready when he called to pick them up, Sophie in a warm sweater and dungarees beneath her coat. Emma wore denims and a soft cotton overshirt. There hadn't been time to put her hair up, but she had washed it quickly and it had dried naturally while she gave Sophie her tea and helped her to dress.

She was satisfied that at least it gleamed healthily, falling in a mass of silky curls to her shoulders.

Daniel gave her a long glance as he helped her into the car, a smouldering heat in his eyes as he took in the way her jeans moulded themselves to the curve of hip and thigh, and when his jaw worked briefly she felt an answering fire leap in her veins. Was she beginning to get under his skin? Good.

He slammed her door shut and went around the car to slide in behind the wheel.

Her heart beat to a crazy tempo, and didn't settle down until they arrived at the fair and she busied herself, setting Sophie down on the grass.

'Can I ride in the big teacup?' Sophie asked, her face lighting up as they approached the rides.

'Of course.'

Daniel helped her onto the seat and made sure the guard chain was in place, before stepping back beside Emma. There was a crowd of people standing by, and Emma was nudged into collision with his hard thigh. His hand settled warmly, possessively, on her hip, and she looked up at him, oddly breathless, her senses reacting in chaotic disarray. They watched the roundabout start up, and waved as Sophie's cup started to circle.

Sophie shouted and they waved again, and when the ride came to an end they wandered around the fairground, letting her try out the merry-go-round, hook a duck to win a cuddly toy and all the other things that caught her attention.

They bought candy floss from a stall and bit into it and let it melt on their tongues. When Emma laughingly complained that her hand was sticky with sugar, Daniel drew her fingers to his mouth and licked them slowly, making her toes curl and her nerve endings sizzle.

An hour or so later, when their arms were full of toys

and posters, and Sophie was yawning widely, they started back to the cottage.

'I'll put her to bed,' Emma murmured, when they had unloaded everything in the kitchen, 'then I'll make us a hot drink. You'll stay, won't you?'

He nodded. 'Go and settle her down for the night.'

He was standing by the table when she came into the living room a few minutes later. He looked so rugged and wonderfully male that her heart skipped a beat, her throat squeezing a little as she walked over to him.

'It was fun tonight,' she murmured. 'I haven't enjoyed a fairground so much since I was a small child.' She smiled up at him and gently leaned against him, savouring the strength of his muscled body, exulting in the flicker of hunger that flared suddenly in the depths of his eyes. She lifted a hand to his arm and felt the coiled tension in the hard muscle, and wonderingly let her fingers explore.

Her fingers moved upwards, trailed over the carved line of his jaw and slid around his neck to tangle in the silky hair at his nape. Her lips parted in soft invitation, and he pulled her to him, his eyes glittering like hot steel.

'Do you have any idea what you're doing?'

Her blue gaze held his. 'I think I'm saying thank you for a lovely evening,' she murmured, and in the next second his mouth met hers, and he was kissing her hungrily, his hands sliding restlessly over her soft, womanly shape.

His kisses lit a flame deep inside her, and her senses registered the hard impact of his strong, muscular frame and the sensual glide of his hands. She returned his kisses, her lips clinging, and threaded her hands through his crisp, dark hair, loving the way he held her close, her body aching with feverish need.

'I've been wanting to do this all night,' he growled softly against her mouth. 'Did you set out to tempt me? Don't you know you're playing with fire?'

'Am I?' She clung to him, feeling dizzy with wanting him. She ran her hands over him, exploring the warm contours of his muscled chest, wanting to touch the bare skin beneath his shirt.

A soft moan escaped her as his hands travelled over her curves, moving with tender possession to claim the soft mound of her breast. Her tender flesh burgeoned against his palm, the delicate nub surging to life beneath his caressing fingers, and she drew in a shuddering breath as her body trembled against his.

His sensuous mouth explored the silky smooth column of her throat, and drifted lower, nuzzling aside the loose fabric of her shirt to lightly graze the gentle slope of her breast.

'Too many clothes,' he whispered huskily. 'I want to kiss you, run my lips over every sweet part of you.'

A honeyed shiver of anticipation ran through her. 'I want you,' she whispered. 'I was wrong to have doubts before. You're such a lovely man, so thoughtful…kind… Just watching you with the children, with Sophie, that shows me what kind of man you are.' She wanted him to be part of her life, sharing in everything with her, body and soul.

He dragged his mouth from her silken flesh, his breathing harsh, uneven, his eyes a dark, smoke grey. 'Don't fall for me, Emma,' he warned in a roughened voice. 'You're a sweet, lovely girl, and I don't want to hurt you—you've been through so much already. Let's just enjoy being together for the moment.'

She shook her head and gave an unsteady little laugh, not sure what to make of what he was saying. 'I think it's too late for that. I've already fallen. Is that such a bad thing?'

He sighed raggedly. 'Bad? No, of course not. But perhaps you're not as sure of your feelings as you imagine. Let's keep things as they are for now—no strings on either side. I know that most women want permanency, commitment—and that's understandable—but it's something I've never been able to give, Emma. It isn't in me to live up to that kind of expectation... I thought you understood that.'

'How could I? You can't mean what you said, surely? You have so much love to give...'

'No,' he said heavily. 'Love is a myth, a fantasy. It isn't real, it doesn't last.'

She drew back a little. 'You can't believe that. You aren't a loner, not deep down inside. You care too much for other people—your father, your patients. I don't believe what you're telling me. You've been hurt...some girlfriend in the past, who didn't deserve you, who made you put up your defences.'

His mouth twisted. 'You've been listening to stories. Everyone gets hurt at some point, but they bounce back. They start to believe in the fantasy again. I don't. I'm a realist, and I don't get taken in by the illusion of what seems like love. People start off with stars in their eyes, and then their dreams get shattered when things start to go wrong.'

'That sounds so bleak, so final. Surely, some day, you'll want more, you'll want a satisfying relationship, a family of your own?'

'It's not going to happen, not for me.' She opened her mouth to protest and he went on quickly, 'I've seen too much suffering, too many children the product of broken homes, to want to inflict that on my own flesh and blood. I saw my own parents' marriage break down, and I've seen the end results of others' in my work.'

He grimaced and placed a hand beneath her jaw, tilting her head a little so that he could look into her eyes.

'That doesn't mean we can't be friends, though, does it? That we can't have fun together, take each day as it comes?'

She stared up at him, her eyes over-bright, holding back the tears that threatened. 'Friends, yes…but you're really talking about an affair, aren't you? A light-hearted flirtation, nothing more than just living for the moment, taking what comes along. I don't know if I'm ready for that just now. I need to think things through. Maybe I shouldn't have let things get out of hand…'

His body tensed. 'No, you shouldn't.' There was a stark edge to the words. 'We should have kept to the original plan, kept a professional distance between us from the start, then this would never have happened. But it's too late now…we have to find a way to deal with this.'

He moved abruptly away from her. 'I think I'd better go. I don't trust myself around you. I'll see you at the surgery,' he muttered, and walked briskly to the door. She watched him leave, a bleak emptiness in her gaze.

Too late, he'd said, and he was right—it *was* too late because she knew now that she loved him, and that was an impossible situation to be in. His heart was closed to love, shut in behind an impenetrable, protective wall, and she didn't know how she could begin to break it down.

She went up to her bedroom and lay down on the bed, dashing away the tears that sprang to her eyes, and buried her head in the pillow and tried to shut out the world.

CHAPTER SEVEN

OVER the next few days they tried to keep out of each other's way. Emma was constantly aware of Daniel, though, and perhaps he was of her, because it felt as though his glance touched her and shifted quickly away whenever they were in a room together.

One morning, before surgery, he reached for a pile of letters just as she leaned over to access the computer. Their fingers touched, and Emma felt the bolt of energy sizzle along her arm.

He snatched his hand back. 'We could do with more workspace.'

'I just need to find an address,' she muttered. She tried to slow down the heavy slam of her heartbeat by concentrating on the computer screen. 'It shouldn't take long.'

He stood to one side while she brought up the information she needed. 'Is Sophie still staying with you?'

'No. Steve came to collect her yesterday. He took us to see a pantomime.'

'You're managing to see her on a fairly regular basis,' he said.

'Yes.' For the moment at least, she was able to spend some time with Sophie. That was the only consolation at the end of the day, and she was making the most of her visits. She didn't know how many more there would be.

Steve might have been thinking along the same lines because he had suggested they could all take a trip over

147

to an ice skating show today, and Emma had agreed to meet them after work.

When Daniel spoke again, he had his mind on business. 'Fran Halloway's husband called a few minutes ago,' he said briskly. 'He says she's not feeling well, and he's worried because she's supposed to be going into hospital tomorrow for the operation. He doesn't want to ring in and cancel it without your approval.'

Emma frowned. 'Did he say what was wrong with her?'

'No. Just that she was feeling low and he wondered if she was coming down with something. He sounded anxious. What procedure is she having tomorrow?'

'An oophorectomy. I explained it to her, and she seemed all right about it. I'd better add her to my list of home visits and find out what's wrong. I don't think she ought to delay things for too long.'

He didn't stay around to debate the issue with her, and she made herself concentrate on the work in hand. It was going to be a major problem, working together in this cool, estranged atmosphere when she longed to be part of his life. He had made it very plain, though, that all he wanted was a light-hearted, uncomplicated affair.

Why couldn't she settle for that? Wouldn't he grow to love her, eventually? But she didn't really think that was very likely. Given his background, she should count herself lucky that he had let her get as close as she had.

With a heavy sigh, she checked through her post and ran through her list of home visits. She tacked Fran on the end, and it was getting on for lunchtime when she eventually stopped by the house.

Tim Halloway let her in. 'She's in the bedroom,' he

said. 'I finally managed to persuade her that she should lie down. She kept insisting that she had such a lot to do, but she was almost in a state of collapse.'

'What has she been doing that was so important?'

'Shopping for groceries and cooking, would you believe it? Stacks of home-made pies and puddings for the freezer. She seems to be afraid I'm going to starve while she's in hospital, and then she started to feel ill and said she couldn't go in. Will you have a word with her, find out what's wrong?'

'I'll do my best.'

Fran looked pale and wretched, and her eyes were puffy, as though she'd been crying.

'Tell me what this is all about,' Emma said, putting an arm around her shoulders. 'What's the matter?'

'You'll think I'm so silly,' Fran said.

'I doubt it.' Emma smiled wryly. 'I've spent a lot of time talking to patients, and nobody's worries are silly. What's the problem?'

'It's just that I don't think I can go through with it. All this while I've kept the appointments and I've gone through with it all, and listened to what everyone has told me, and put up a cheerful front...but I'm really scared inside.'

'What are you afraid of? The operation itself, or afterwards?'

Fran sniffed and reached for a hanky. 'Both, I think. I keep thinking what might go wrong, or that they'll find something nasty.' She bit her lip and blew her nose. 'I've driven Tim mad this last week, cleaning the house and shopping and stacking the fridge and freezer, but I wanted to make sure he's got everything he needs if anything should happen to me.'

'Why do you think something might happen to you?' Emma asked gently.

Fran flapped her hands weakly. 'I know I'm sounding feeble but, you see, I lost my gran last year. She went into hospital for an operation and she had a stroke and died, and I just can't stop thinking about it.'

'Oh, you poor girl.' Emma gave her a hug. 'That's really sad. I can understand how you must be feeling but, you know, it doesn't mean that anything like that is going to happen to you. You're young, and you've kept yourself relatively fit. This isn't a terribly difficult operation that you're going to have, and when it's all finished and done with you'll feel so much better. It isn't really something that you can simply ignore.

'I expect you're feeling all the more low right now because you've exhausted yourself with all the cleaning and so on. Try to relax a bit, and think about what you're going to do when you come out of hospital.'

Emma paused. 'Didn't you say you wanted to start a family at some point? Isn't that something to think about and look forward to? Can you talk it over with Tim? He probably needs you to share all this with him.'

Fran nodded and blew her nose again. 'I expect you're right. I've been so busy I haven't talked to him properly.'

Emma smiled. 'Well, you can start to remedy that right now, can't you? And I can give you something to help you get a good night's sleep. Is Tim going to take you to the hospital tomorrow?'

'Yes, he said he would.'

Emma spent another half-hour or so at the house, having a cup of tea with them and satisfying herself that Fran was calmer and in a better frame of mind.

Tim saw her to the door when she was ready to go.

'Thanks for coming out to see her,' he said. 'I knew something was wrong, but she wouldn't talk to me about it. She just kept it bottled up inside.'

'I think she'll be all right now,' Emma murmured. 'Make sure she gets some rest, and if there's any problem give me a ring.'

'I will.'

Emma made a note to ring the hospital and talk to Sister Matthews on the admitting ward. She was an old friend, and she would look after Fran well and talk to her about her fears.

Emma went back to Woodhouse. The afternoon appointments took longer than she expected, and when she glanced at her watch later in the day she knew that she would have to hurry to be ready in time for the ice show. She quickly dealt with the pile of papers that had mounted up in her wire tray, then she hurried along to the main door, checking her bag for her keys.

She collided with someone strong, warm, and solid, and looked up in surprise, winded by the soft crush of the impact.

Daniel steadied her.

'You're in a hurry,' he said. 'What's all the rush about? Problems?'

She shook her head. 'Not really,' she said breathlessly, her nervous system doing crazy somersaults in response to his nearness. 'I'm just late. Steve's picking me up in half an hour, and I'm nowhere near ready.'

'Oh, I see.' He let go of her. 'I won't keep you, then.' His expression was shuttered again, and she wished they could go back to the friendly intimacy they had shared before.

'The trainee will be in tomorrow, by the way,' he added. 'I shall need to spend a fair amount of time talking to her about how she's coping, but if there's any problem you need to see me about concerning the patients, we'll sort it out as it arises.'

He was being very formal with her, and already he was moving away from her towards Reception. Bleakly, she watched him go.

She didn't get a chance to speak to him at all next day. The trainee doctor was at the surgery, as he'd said, and all his time was taken up in conference with her. Nothing cropped up that she needed to consult him over, and she simply concentrated on her work.

There had been no call from Tim so she took it that Fran had gone into hospital as planned, and she asked Alison to check up on things there later.

The following day, at the finish of early evening surgery, she was about to leave for home when a call came in from Mrs Harding's husband.

'Sandra's had a fall,' he said anxiously. 'She's in a lot of pain and I think her leg might be broken.'

'I'll come over and take a look,' Emma promised.

Daniel had come out of his room and heard what was going on. 'I'll come with you,' he said. 'Drop your car off at the cottage and we'll take mine. You can fill me in on the day's events as we go. We haven't had a chance to get together so far.'

'Did you want to talk to me? I thought you might be trying to avoid me, if the truth be known.'

He grimaced at that. 'It hasn't been easy for either of us this last week,' he said gruffly.

'No, it hasn't.' Perhaps it would get easier with time, but for the moment, out of sheer defensiveness, they kept the conversation to work-related matters.

Mrs Harding's leg was broken, as Frank had suspected, and needed splinting. Daniel went to search in the boot of his car for a board, while Emma gave Sandra an injection to relieve the pain.

'How on earth did you manage to do this?' Daniel asked, when he came back.

'I fell over the edge of the path. Stupid, wasn't it? I never thought a simple thing like that would break it.'

'Your bones may be less dense than they used to be,' he murmured. 'After the menopause a lot of women do suffer fractures because of osteoporosis. But we'll know more about that after it's been X-rayed. If it is osteoporosis, you could think about hormone replacement therapy to stop the condition worsening, but for the moment let's just get you comfortable. I think we should get you to the hospital to let the doctors look at it properly and get you plastered.'

'On the NHS?' Frank Harding remarked with a grin. 'Make mine a Scotch!'

'You should be so lucky,' Daniel chuckled. 'Come on, let's get her settled in the car as best we can. You drive and I'll follow in my car.'

'You won't want to wait around with us,' Sandra said, looking pale but less tense now that the pain was receding. 'It's late already, and I could be at the hospital half the night.'

'I'll stay and visit my father a while, and then check on you,' Daniel said. 'I expect they'll show you how to use a pair of crutches once the plaster's dry.'

He turned to Emma. 'Would you like to come along and visit? You said you'd like to talk to him when he was feeling better.'

Warmth sprang up in her chest. 'I'd love to.' He was including her in his plans at last, and it gave her some small hope for the future. He might not love her, but just being with him was enough for now.

They left Sandra and Frank in the A & E department, and went on to the stroke unit, where they found John Maitland sitting in an armchair at the side of his bed, listening to a book on cassette that Daniel had taken in for him.

He was pleased to see them both, and struggled to switch off the tape. Emma instinctively wanted to help him, but stopped herself, realising that the more he could manage for himself, the better the long-term result.

'You look much brighter than the last time I saw you,' she said. 'How are you feeling?'

'Better every day,' he said slowly. He had been having speech therapy, and it had clearly done him some good.

Daniel added some fresh fruit to his father's bowl, and smiled at him. 'You're doing very well,' he said. 'Well enough to flirt with the nurses, from what I hear.' He gave a wry grin. 'I heard about the offer to wine and dine them. You'll have a problem if they all accept!'

'Good excuse for a party, though!' John gave a husky laugh.

'And all the more reason for you to get back on your feet. Have the physios been helping you to walk?'

'They give it a go every day. Haven't got all my strength back just yet,' John said. 'Still a bit shaky.'

'It'll come. Don't worry.'

They sat with him for a while, talking, telling him what had happened to Sandra and reading aloud bits from the newspaper that Daniel had brought in with him. Then the door opened and a woman walked into the room.

Daniel tensed a fraction, but John's face broke into

a faintly lopsided smile. There was still some remaining weakness after the paralysis of his facial muscles.

Even before the introductions, Emma guessed that the woman must be Daniel's mother. She had the same dark hair and the bone structure of her face was cleanly moulded like Daniel's, her eyes the same intense grey.

'Katherine.' John lifted a shaky hand and she went over to him and clasped it in her own, kissing him lightly on the cheek. 'I wasn't sure whether you'd come.'

'I said I would, didn't I? I've been sorting out the news for you from the business. They're all getting on just fine. You've got some good managers in place there. You should stop worrying and let them get on with their jobs.' She handed him a package. 'I brought some letters in for you from the Regency.'

'I don't know if they can cope,' he began.

'You do,' she admonished him. 'Daniel's already told you that they were coping.'

She glanced at her son, and he simply looked back at her, his mouth firm, his jaw set. It was a look she must have seen many times because her mouth made an odd shape, and then she turned back to her ex-husband.

'It's time you relaxed and let them get on with it. You're near to retirement age now, and you should be thinking of yourself and how you can enjoy your leisure time.'

'They need me to keep an eye on them.'

'From time to time, maybe. You've worked too hard over the years. You've worried too much and put too much into it.'

'I did it for you.' He frowned and reached slowly and carefully for a glass of juice from his bedside table.

Katherine shook her head. 'You might have told yourself that. But you loved it really, in the beginning. You were obsessed by it—the success, the thrill of seeing it grow. It took over and there was no time left for me. You let it take over.'

John put down the now-empty glass, and she said, 'Here, let me get you some fresh juice. There's a cassette tape among the things I brought in. Why don't you have a listen to it?'

Katherine retrieved his jug from the table and went over to the sink at the far side of the room to refill it. John turned his attention to the package of letters and the tape, and just as Emma was helping him slide the cassette into the machine, giving him the headset to listen through, a nurse came into the room.

'I need to take you over to the nursing station and organise your medication, John,' she told him. 'Sorry to disturb you, but we'll have you back in a minute or two.'

When John had gone from the room, Daniel went over to his mother and said, 'You shouldn't have criticised him like that. He needs to be calm if he's to get well. This is hardly the time or place to be bringing up past problems.'

'It's exactly the time and place,' Katherine retorted. 'That's why he's here—because he couldn't let go. The tension just went on building up until something exploded.'

'You didn't stay around when he was going through all the stress of seeing his business take off. You weren't concerned then. You left him to cope on his own. Why should you be bothered now?'

'Do you think I didn't want to stay? What makes you think he was on his own? You think you have all the answers, but you saw it through a child's eyes. You didn't know what I had to deal with. You still don't see any of it. Your stepmother came on the scene pretty quickly, don't you think?'

Daniel looked taken aback for a moment, but he recovered swiftly. 'You can't simply turn things around to suit yourself. You walked out on both of us.'

'You think I walked out on you, but I didn't want it to be that way. It wasn't an easy decision to make.'

His mouth hardened. 'You made it, though.' He turned away from her and walked back across the room to Emma. 'I think we should head back to the A & E. I'll go and find Dad and tell him we have to go.'

Emma nodded, but John was already on his way back.

Daniel spoke quietly to him for a few minutes, then gently squeezed his shoulder. 'I have to go now,' he said, 'but I'll stop by tomorrow. You take care.'

Emma collected her things and went over to Katherine. 'Will you be staying over here for long, or do you have to be back at work? I heard that you're a journalist—I think I may have read some of your articles.'

'I'm not working now. I reckon I've earned my retirement, and I just plan on settling down in some nice little house with roses round the door.' She smiled faintly.

Emma intercepted a look from Daniel and said her goodbyes. 'We have to go and check on Sandra,' she said. 'She'll probably be just about ready to go home now. They weren't too busy down in A & E.'

Out in the corridor, she glanced quickly at Daniel's shuttered features. 'Are you being a bit hard on your mother after all this time? She can't be all bad, can she?

At least she's trying to help your father on the road to recovery. I get the feeling she wants to talk to you properly, to explain. Wouldn't it be for the best if you could try to meet her halfway, instead of arguing with her?'

He shrugged. 'There's never been much love lost between us. She had a choice back then. She decided to go away and leave me, and things have never been right between us since then.'

'Only because you don't make an effort to sort things out. She's your flesh and blood, and I think she still cares about you and your father—or why else is she here? Some time you're going to have to face up to things, Daniel. You've built a wall around your emotions, but you can't lock yourself behind it for ever. It isn't healthy. You won't let yourself trust anyone, and in the end that will destroy you because no one can live in isolation like that. You'll never be whole again until you break the barrier down, and the only way to do that is to talk to your mother properly and learn to forgive a little.'

'I don't need lessons in psychology from you, Emma,' he said through gritted teeth.

Emma winced. It hurt her to see him suffering inside, closing his mind on a problem that wasn't going to go away until he tackled it head on.

They went over to A & E, and Emma went to speak to the doctor in charge of Sandra's case and check on the X-rays.

'There weren't any complications,' the doctor said. 'It was a straightforward break so we were able to get on with plastering it. It does look as though there's a degree of osteoporosis so she'll need to be careful to avoid more falls. She's in some pain now so I think the

injection must be wearing off. I'll prescribe some an-
algesics for her.'

Emma went back to Sandra. 'The doctor is going to
give you something for the pain,' she said. 'It appears
that your bones aren't as strong as they might be, so
when you're feeling up to it come along to the surgery
and we'll have a chat about that and see what we can
do to boost you. You might want to try HRT because
that might help your body utilise the calcium in your
diet to strengthen the bone.'

'I'm not sure,' Sandra said. 'I've heard bad reports
about the side-effects.'

Emma nodded. 'It's true, there may be problems as-
sociated with HRT, and we may need to look at different strategies, but we can talk about that later. For now
just let's get you home, shall we?'

They found a wheelchair for her, and Emma helped
Frank adjust it so that Sandra's leg was supported. Then
they all went out to the car, and helped to get her settled
for the journey home. Once the couple were on their
way, Daniel drove Emma back to the cottage.

'Do you want to come in for a while?' she asked,
when they pulled up outside her house.

He studied her for a long moment, then leaned towards her, his gaze settling on her soft mouth. The light
from the streetlamp shed a golden glow over the interior
of the car, highlighting the firm line of his jaw. Just
looking at him, it made her mouth go dry. He looked
incredibly male, and she was driven by a crazy urge to
reach out and touch her hand to his face and explore
all the ridges and hollows with her fingers.

'I don't think so,' he murmured, breaking into her
wayward thoughts. He eased away from her. 'It might
not be such a good idea.'

'But—'

'I need to be on my own for a while,' he said. 'I need to think things through.'

'Can't I help?'

'No. This is something I have to work out for myself. Go in, Emma.'

There was a finality to his tone, and she turned and fumbled with the doorhandle, getting out of the car and walking quickly over to the house. She didn't look back.

Steve rang couple of days later and asked her over for an evening with him and Sophie, and at least she could look forward to that. He still hadn't heard about the job, and Emma didn't know whether to be relieved or not. She felt as though a black tide was rolling inexorably towards her, and she was trying to push it back with her fingers.

Emma's list for surgery next day was over-full, and from a swift glance around the waiting room she saw that Tracy Walker was there, tearful, holding her hand to her stomach and looking as though she was in pain again.

'That makes several visits in a matter of months,' she murmured to Daniel, who was busy checking his own list. 'It's obviously a recurrent problem, but I just can't find any clue at the moment as to what's causing it. It's just knowing how to unravel the puzzle.'

'Family background?' Daniel commented, lifting a brow.

'Maybe.'

Tracy had stopped crying by the time she came into Emma's room with her mother, and she allowed Emma to gently examine her. As Emma had expected, she found nothing to point to any physical problem.

'Shouldn't she have some more tests?' her mother asked. 'We need to know why she keeps getting this pain and do something about it.'

'You're right, Mrs Walker, we do need to get to the bottom of it, but Tracy has had all the tests necessary, and so far they have proved negative. I think we should have a chat about it for a few minutes while Tracy plays with the toys in Reception. I'll ask Alison to keep an eye on her, if that's all right with you.'

Under normal circumstances she would have let the child play in her room, but she had a feeling that Tracy's ears were more sharply tuned than they had recognised, and it might be better if they were able to talk freely.

When the little girl had gone off happily with Alison, she asked Mrs Walker if she could think of anything that had happened to upset Tracy recently.

'Nothing,' she answered blankly. 'Are you saying that she's making it up? That there isn't any pain?'

'No, not at all. The pain is very real, I'm sure. Pain doesn't always have a physical cause, though. Imagine, for instance, how an adult might feel if she gets wedding nerves, or has to go for a job interview. The stress can cause all sorts of symptoms, like sweating, palpitations, feeling sick, or having to run to the toilet. I think Tracy's pain might be triggered in a similar way—by stress of some kind—though we don't really know what just yet. You said she was happy at school and with her friends. Is that still the case?'

'Well, yes, I think so. Whenever she tells me about what happens there, she seems happy enough. But she didn't want to go the other day, and the teacher said she was a bit anxious in the afternoons sometimes, waiting for me to come and fetch her. I don't know why. I haven't been able to find out.'

'It does sound as though something's troubling her,' Emma said. 'Is she sleeping all right?'

Mrs Walker chewed on her lip. 'She has had one or two nightmares lately. I thought perhaps it was something she'd seen on TV.'

'It's possible, though if she's troubled at school as well it points to something more than that. Is there anything happening within the family that might be worrying her?'

'I don't think so. There's only me at home really. My husband's working away a lot of the time.'

'Does he come home at the weekends? Do you think she might be missing him?'

'He doesn't always get home. To be honest, we've not been getting on too well, and he's stayed over in digs a few times. We were talking about splitting up— but Tracy doesn't know that. We've mostly talked about it after she's gone to bed.'

Emma was doubtful. 'I wouldn't be too sure that she doesn't know. Children are very good at listening when parents think they're busy with other things. It might be worth finding out what she thinks about Daddy being away from home—in a gentle, tactful way. She might not tell you all at once, but you could broach the subject in a variety of ways over time.'

Mrs Walker nodded, frowning a little, deep in thought. Then she got to her feet, saying, 'You've given me something to think about, Doctor. I'll have a word with her.'

She went out, and Emma rang for the next patient.

As the day wore on she started to feel decidedly weary, and it must have shown because when she finally

emerged from her room late in the afternoon, Daniel
said, 'You look as though you've had a bad day.'

'I can't say I'm sorry it's over,' she told him with a
rueful grin. 'I've had two or three tricky cases to deal
with, and the list seemed longer than usual today.'

'You sound as though you need a change of scene.
We could go out somewhere maybe. I know a nice little
restaurant we might try.'

Emma blinked, then shook her head. 'Thanks, but I
can't,' she said with an inward twinge of regret. 'I'm
supposed to be going over to Steve's house for a meal.
He's learned his way around a kitchen these last few
months, and I think he wants to impress me with his
latest concoction.' She gave a little laugh, but he didn't
answer her smile and his eyes were dark and smokily
grey.

'You seem to be getting on better with him now.'

'I am. He's trying hard to do the right thing.'

'Well, anyway, try to enjoy your evening.'

'I will. Thanks.'

Daniel collected his jacket and went out through the
main door to the car park. Watching him go, she
thought wistfully of how the evening might have been.
Then, suppressing a sigh, she quickly sifted through the
papers in her tray and decided they could safely be left
until morning.

As it was, the meal Steve cooked was delicious, and
she enjoyed the time she spent with Sophie.

There was still no news of the job he had applied for,
and she pushed all thoughts of it to the back of her
mind.

The next day seemed as busy as ever. She did the
home visits, and called in on Sandra to see how she was
coping with the plaster cast.

'It's so heavy,' she complained. 'I'm supposed to go back in a couple of weeks to have them check it. I just hope they'll lighten it a bit.'

'We'll have to wait and see,' Emma murmured. 'The main thing is to X-ray the leg again and see how it's healing.' She inspected Sandra's toes, peeping out from the end of the cast. 'Your circulation looks good, anyway. How are you feeling in general? Are the painkillers helping?'

'Yes. I was hoping I could do without them by now, but I can't get to sleep at night unless I've taken a couple. It's worse than toothache.'

'At least she doesn't have to do the housework,' Frank cut in. 'Fine way to get out of it, I must say!'

'I'm sure she makes a good forewoman, though,' Emma said, smiling. 'She'll know just what needs doing and how to keep you busy!'

'Too right, she does. Don't I know it?'

'You'd better watch your step, my lad,' Sandra said. 'I might decide to let you carry on once I'm back on my feet. You can do the housework here while I concentrate on John's place.'

Emma left them still exchanging banter, and went into Woodhouse to prepare for the afternoon appointments.

She spent a few minutes talking to Jane in Reception, until Daniel arrived and asked the nurse if she would help him with a rheumatoid patient who had come for an injection.

Emma scanned the notes in her tray. After a while the phone rang, and because Alison was busy for a moment in the office she answered it herself.

'Emma?' Steve said. 'I've just heard about the job I applied for. It's mine. Isn't it great news?'

Emma slowly absorbed what he had said. Even though she had been half expecting it, the reality still came as a shock to her and she didn't know how to respond.

'Emma? Are you still there?'

She took in a deep breath. 'Yes. I'm still here. When do you have to leave?'

'In three weeks' time. There's so much I shall need to arrange before then. All the packing, and deciding what needs to be crated up and shipped out. The house to be let—or put on the market—accommodation to arrange out there, and what to do about Sophie. I'll have to check with the agencies for day care over there.'

Emma hardly heard the rest of what he was saying. Part of her had hoped all along that he wouldn't get the job, that Sophie would be staying. And now she had to face up to the facts.

She murmured something in reply, and Daniel appeared at her side as she put the receiver down.

'What's wrong?' he asked. He came and stood close to her, his grey eyes searching her pale features.

'He's going away,' she muttered. 'Steve's going away. He's going to live abroad.' She blinked hard, trying to dash away the film of tears that threatened to blur her vision.

'You're worried about Sophie?'

She nodded. 'I'll miss her. I've grown too used to having her around.' She bit her lip. Too many things were going wrong.

Why was it that the people she cared about most were in the end lost to her? Sophie was going away, and Daniel…he was there at her side, but in reality he was lost to her as well. He didn't want her in the way that mattered. She had fallen for a man who didn't believe in love. The future spread out before her, and it looked bleak and empty.

CHAPTER EIGHT

DANIEL was still watching Emma, worried about her reaction. Then he said, 'Come through to the staff lounge. We'll talk about it there.'

He was showing concern for her, just as he might for a patient, but she wanted more than that from him. More than he was able to provide. She shook her head. 'I'll be all right. I must get ready for surgery.' Then she swivelled away from the desk and hurried to her room.

All along, she had known there was a strong possibility that Sophie might be taken away from her, but she had deliberately pushed it to the back of her mind, had made plans to have her stay over at the weekends. She hadn't wanted to accept that Daniel might be right, that Steve was the one who was ultimately responsible for his child.

Why couldn't she think what to do? This last year she had come through so much, had tried to get her life back on track, and include Sophie in it, and now things were coming unstuck again. There must be some way around the situation, something she could do.

She went over to the washbasin in the corner of the room and splashed her skin with water. Carefully, she dried her face and repaired her make-up, readying herself to cope with the afternoon ahead. There were patients to be seen, and she couldn't keep them waiting any longer.

Somehow she managed to keep her mind on work and get through the rest of the day. When the appointments had all been attended to, she went along to Reception and started on her paperwork, signing all the letters and repeat prescriptions that Alison had put on one side for her.

Fran's operation had gone smoothly, and she made arrangements for the nurse to call and check on her condition on her release from hospital. Stewart was due to have his surgery in a couple of days' time.

She had almost finished her work when she was startled to see Steve come into the office.

'Are you all right?' he asked. 'You sounded a bit odd on the phone, and I thought I'd come along and see you.'

'I'm fine,' she said. 'I'm pleased for you about the job, really.'

He looked at her thoughtfully, then said quietly, 'You could come with me, you know. I'd like you to. Can we go somewhere and talk about this?'

She swallowed hard, then nodded briefly, placing the sheaf of papers in her tray. 'OK. I've finished here for the day.'

They went towards the door together, and it was only then that she saw that Daniel had come into the room. She thought he was going to say something, but he stayed silent, standing aside to let them pass, and as she went by him she felt his body tense. She loved him, and yet it seemed as though there was a great chasm between them that could not be bridged.

She didn't see him again until she arrived at Woodhouse the next morning, and then he was leaving the office, his expression preoccupied.

Her heart sank as she watched him go. She needed to talk to him. After last night's meeting with Steve she was still undecided what to do, and she would have liked to talk it through with Daniel. He had offered help before, but maybe he felt she had rejected him, been too abrupt. Or perhaps it was simply that he was leaving because something had cropped up.

'Has something happened?' she asked Jane.

Jane pulled a wry face. 'His father's coming out of hospital.'

She was startled. 'But that's good news, isn't it?'

'I'm not exactly sure. He says it's too soon, that he'll need hand-rails and so on to help him get around and the workmen haven't finished installing them yet.'

'He'll need more than that. He should have someone to help him at the house. Mrs Harding won't be able to do it for quite a while.'

'True, but Mrs Maitland is going to be looking after him. She's going to be living in— I'm not sure what Daniel feels about that.'

Emma's eyes widened. No wonder he had looked preoccupied. 'Oh, I see,' she murmured. 'Perhaps I'll get a chance to talk to him about it later.'

She didn't get the opportunity until after morning surgery, but as soon as she was able she put her head around the door of his room.

'Is this a good time to talk?'

Daniel looked up from his notes and leaned back in his chair. 'That depends. Is it about your meeting with Steve? I heard him ask if you would go with him. If you've decided to do that, and you've come to tell me you want to break your contract, then, no, it isn't. Nor is it ever likely to be.'

Emma frowned. Was that the reason for his cool, slightly guarded response? Because he thought she might break her contract? Not because she might be going away… Her stomach made an uneasy flipover.

'I... No...that wasn't it, exactly.'

His grey eyes scanned her face keenly. 'It wasn't?'

'I haven't decided what to do yet,' she confessed. 'I keep thinking there must be another way—but I just haven't been able to come up with a reasonable alternative yet.' She paused, thinking it through. Daniel frowned, and she straightened up. 'Enough of my troubles. I really came to say that I heard about your father coming out of hospital. Can I help you to get him settled at the house? Is there anything he needs? Maybe we could have lunch together and talk. We haven't had the chance lately.'

He shook his head. 'I'm having lunch with the trainee today to go over some of the things that came up during surgery. Then we have to do the home calls. As to my dad, I'll manage, thanks.'

'OK.' She kept the disappointment out of her voice. He was busy, and it was perfectly reasonable that he wanted to deal with things on his own, but she couldn't help feeling just a little pushed out, and it hurt. 'Just let me know if there's anything I can do,' she said.

For the rest of the day, she kept her head down, got on with her clinic and did what she could to keep her problems at bay. If she thought about what the future held, it brought up a welter of uneasy choices, and for the present she tried to lose herself in hard work.

Stewart went in for his operation and was transferred to Intensive Care immediately afterwards until his condition stabilised. Emma went to see him, and spoke to his wife, making sure that she was coping adequately. Her asthma was troublesome, but at least she was managing to keep it under control.

When she saw Fran, she discovered that her wound

was healing nicely, and she was in great spirits after the ordeal.

'I was such a wimp,' she said. 'The nurses were so good to me, but I was still scared, and when they wheeled me down to Theatre I kept thinking, this is it, then. It all ends here—at least Tim will be all right for a while without me. There's plenty of food in the house so he won't starve for a few weeks.' She grinned broadly. 'And then when I came round from the anaesthetic and found I was all right, it was just as though the sun had come out. It felt glorious!'

'I'm glad you're feeling better,' Emma said. At least Fran had something to be happy about. She wished her own life could be as uncomplicated. She pushed the thought away and gave Fran a smile. 'The dressing can come off in a couple of days. You're doing very well.'

Emma drove back to the surgery and was surprised to find Katherine Maitland waiting there to see her.

'Did you want Daniel?' she asked. 'I think he's out with the trainee doing the afternoon home visits.'

Katherine shook her head. 'I've tried talking to him, but I don't feel that I'm getting anywhere. I don't know how to get through to him properly. He seems so withdrawn.' She hesitated. 'I wondered if you might have a word on my behalf. He might listen to you. He seems to care very much about you.'

'I wouldn't say that, exactly. I don't think I have much sway with him,' Emma commented. 'I doubt if he will listen to me either.' She sighed, then added, 'Come on through to my room for a chat. I'll make us some coffee.'

They took their drinks with them, and Katherine toyed with her spoon as she said bleakly, 'I only want to help his father. I could do so much to make his life easier, but Daniel seemed annoyed that he was coming out of hospital—perhaps he objects to me looking after him. You'd think after all this time… He thinks I deliberately rejected him, and I know he's never forgiven me, but it wasn't like that. I always loved him, and his father.'

'But you did leave them? Something went wrong with your marriage?'

Katherine's mouth moved shakily. 'John had this dream when we were first married. He wanted to own his own hotel, and he worked very hard to build up the capital. He put everything he had into it. It had to be perfect, and he vetted everything—the decoration, the furnishings, the food, the staff. It was a great success, of course, but that was just the start. He wanted more, and the more his ambition grew, the less time he had for me.

'I was lonely, I suppose. I tried to make a career for myself in journalism, and that was very hard because I was competing in what was very much a man's world.' She pressed her lips together briefly, then sipped her coffee.

'Then Daniel came along, and I wanted to be a good mother to him, but it was difficult for me, being at home again with just a small child for company. It seemed to highlight how little John was around. He was busy going here and there, setting up new premises, and in the end I decided to go back to work. At first it was just part time because I tried to compromise between work and being a mother. But I began to make a name for myself as a journalist, and I worked on some TV assignments. I had to make arrangements for Daniel when I had to work away, and after a while the assignments were for longer and longer periods.'

She swallowed more coffee, then put her cup down, and Emma could see that her hand was trembling.

'It's ironic, really,' Katherine went on, 'but round about this time John was finding things easier. The business was set up and running smoothly, and he had more time on his hands so he was able to look after Daniel. They became very close.' She winced, then sighed.

'I started to suspect that John was having an affair. This great split was growing in my marriage, and I didn't know how to put things right. Then I was sent on a long assignment and when I came back there was this other woman on the scene, and John and I—we rowed a lot.'

She pulled in a shaky breath. 'We decided to separate, and I thought in the end it would be best if Daniel stayed with his father. I had to carry on working to support myself—though John would have been very generous if I had let him, but I needed to be independent and make my own way. I couldn't take Daniel with me. A lot of the work I did was in danger spots all over the world.' She paused.

'So, I lost him then. I made arrangements for him to come and stay with me between assignments, but he refused to come and he was awkward when I went to visit him. He was convinced I had left him behind because I didn't want him, and nothing I could say would persuade him otherwise. He withdrew from me, physically and mentally. I was so unhappy. I'd lost my son, my marriage was a mess. At first I cried endlessly, but that was how it was, and I've never been able to get close to Daniel since.'

'You didn't tell him you were hurt by his father's affair?'

Katherine shook her head. 'He was just a child. I didn't want to blacken his father in his eyes.'

'So he might have believed you were leaving him behind in order to concentrate on your career? He didn't see any of this from your point of view?'

'I suppose not.'

Emma put her hand on Katherine's. 'He's not a child any more, but he still has all that hurt locked up inside him. You have to tell him everything, just as you've told it to me.'

Katherine's eyes were bleak. 'But how, when he won't let me near him?'

'You'll be looking after John, won't you? Staying at the house? Daniel will need to visit his father and you're going to be there, too, aren't you? You just have to persevere. Eventually he might start to see your side of things.'

Katherine gave her a weak smile. 'Perhaps you're right. Thank you for listening to me. You've been very kind.'

'If I get the chance to talk to him on your behalf, I will,' Emma promised, when she saw Katherine out some time later. She couldn't hazard a guess as to when that would be likely, but she would do what she could.

She still had to make up her mind what to do about her own future, and it wasn't getting any easier. Sophie knew that her daddy was going to work somewhere else, but she wasn't altogether sure what that meant.

Emma went to see them again, and at bedtime Sophie said, 'Come and tuck me in, Emmy, and read me a story. I wish you would stay here, then you could read to me every day. Will you stay, please?'

Emma gave her a cuddle and struggled to find the right words. What could she say? I'm sorry, but you have to go with your daddy, and we might not see each other again for a long time?

She swallowed against the great lump in her throat and said huskily, 'I'll read you a story now, and stay with you until you've gone to sleep. Then, tomorrow, you're going to the nursery to play with your friends, aren't you, while I go to work?' She settled her in bed, then opened the book and began to read.

Sophie was distracted by that, for a while, but when she snuggled down under the covers, she said, 'Tell Daddy I want you to stay.' A yawn escaped her. 'Tell him I want you to stop here every day.'

Emma kissed her cheek and smoothed her silky curls. 'Go to sleep, sweetheart. I'll talk to Daddy.'

Steve was waiting at the door when she quietly slipped out of the room a moment later.

'She loves you,' he said. 'You've been like a mother to her. I thought I could handle bringing her up on my own, but it's more difficult than I believed possible. She misses her mother. She needs you.'

Back at Woodhouse next morning, Daniel was talking to Mrs Walker, and Emma wondered if another problem had come up.

'Oh, no, there's no problem,' Mrs Walker said. 'I just called in on my way back from taking Tracy to school. I thought you'd like to know that I found out what the trouble was.'

Emma was intrigued. 'You did? What was it?'

'She'd been listening to her dad and me arguing, and she knew that he was thinking of leaving us. Somehow she had got it into her head that if he was going away, then I might leave her as well. That's why she's been so anxious at school lately. She was worried I might not be coming to pick her up.'

'Poor little thing,' Emma said, thinking of all the unhappiness the young girl had been through. 'You've talked it over with her, then, and reassured her?'

'I have. I'm not sure that she completely believes I'm staying yet, but I'll keep on telling her until she feels secure again.'

'That's the best thing you can do,' Emma said. 'I'm really glad that you managed to sort it all out.'

When Mrs Walker had gone, Daniel went back to sifting through his post and then started towards his room. Emma picked up her surgery list and followed him.

'I'm glad she found out what the trouble was.'

'So am I.' He pushed open his door, and she went after him into his room and sat on the edge of the desk.

'Is your father home now? How is he?'

'He went home yesterday. He's going to find it difficult for a while, but at least he's walking now, albeit shakily. The hand-rails are all in place at any rate.'

'Your mother's going to be there to take care of him, isn't she? That must be good for his morale.'

'Maybe. But she left him in the lurch once before and I can't be sure she won't decide she's had enough and go off again.'

'I don't think she'll do that. Before, there was another woman hovering in the background, ready to step into her shoes, and that must have hurt her badly. She still cares about your father.'

'Does she? If she hadn't been so eager to pursue her career in the first place, she might have had more time for my dad. My stepmother might never have been able to step into her shoes.'

'I don't think it was as clear-cut as that,' Emma said quickly. 'I've talked to her, and I know that she loves both of you, and that she wants to talk to you, but you're not making it easy for her. You've built this wall around yourself, and you won't let anyone get through. You're keeping your emotions wound up tight inside you, and that's not doing you any good at all.'

'Are you any better at dealing with personal problems? Can you honestly say you weren't thinking of abandoning your career at a moment's notice to go with Sophie? That would be a crazy thing to do, surely?'

'Would it? You know how much I care about her.'

'You think she's all-important now, but what's going to happen when you meet a man you want to share your life with? Where will she come on your list of priorities then?'

Her mouth wavered. Hadn't she already met that man? How could he not know how she felt about him?

'Do you think I'm so fickle that I can simply ignore her needs?' she said huskily. 'She's tiny and vulnerable. She lost her mother, and I have always been there for her, loving her, taking her mother's place, doing whatever I could to make her happy. How will she react if Steve takes her away and I'm no longer there? I need to find a solution. Steve's coming round to the cottage tonight, and I still haven't come up with an answer. I don't know what to do.' She only had to recall the soft little arms around her neck, and Sophie's gentle plea to stay with her, to feel her insides melt. She could not bear to think of Sophie being unhappy.

'You'll be able to go over and visit. Steve might bring her back here from time to time.'

'But not very often.'

He frowned. 'She's not your child. Why should you care so much?'

Emma pressed her lips together. 'Is it so hard to understand? I helped to nurture her. I held her in my arms and fed her when she was a baby. I changed her nappy, I bathed her. I love her just as much as if she was my own child.'

He was quiet, and she said softly, 'You had a bad experience, and it's coloured your judgement, made you blind to other possibilities. Subconsciously, you expect all women to choose selfishly when it comes to a clash between their own needs and those of their children. But your case was exceptional. It doesn't happen that way very often, and you were unlucky. You need to find out why it happened and come to terms with it.'

'You sound so sure of yourself.' He stared at her. 'A wall, you said. I've built a wall around myself to keep everyone out.'

'I was trying to make you see how much you might be missing. I know your mother has tried to talk to you, to explain her side of things. I'm sure she cares deeply... I feel it instinctively, but you haven't given her a proper chance—you've shut her out for so long.'

'It was all over a long time ago.'

'It's buried maybe. But not forgotten. It still has the power to influence the way you think. You could at least talk to your mother...properly, without putting up a barrier. Listen to what she has to say and try to look at things from her point of view, through the eyes of someone whose marriage was falling apart. And then take a look at the rest of the world and see if you haven't had a jaundiced view of the way people behave.'

His mouth twisted, and he turned at a knock on the door. Jane came into the room.

'Oh, I'm sorry, Daniel. I didn't know you were busy. I've just finished doing the blood tests, and Mrs Martin is first on your list.'

'OK. Thanks. We've finished here. You can tell Alison to send her in.'

Emma glanced swiftly at him, and he said quietly, 'I'm sorry—I'd better see her right away. Mrs Martin's anxious about some results and I need to put her mind at rest.'

She nodded, and he switched on the computer to access the patient's records, his mind reverting to work. She followed Jane out of the room and went to deal with her own patients.

The morning passed quickly, and she tried to push away thoughts of her conversation with Daniel because they were having a disastrous effect on her concentration.

In the afternoon Emma checked her post and saw that Stewart Jackson was out of Intensive Care now and making a good recovery. He would spend the next few weeks getting his strength back, and then he would need to attend the physiotherapy department so that he could be shown how to take gentle exercise to get himself properly fit.

Her hypertension clinic went smoothly, and she finished work in reasonable time to go home and freshen up for the evening ahead.

She needed to feel prepared, and wanted something to lift her spirits. She put on a soft wool sweater that felt good against her skin, and a gently swathed skirt that flowed lightly around her legs as she walked. It helped to make her feel a little better.

The doorbell rang and she hurried to answer it.

It wasn't Steve at the door, though, but Daniel, looking vibrantly sexy and sinfully male in grey trousers that accentuated the long line of his legs and a dark shirt that drew her gaze to his firmly muscled arms and chest.

'Shall I go away again or can I come in?' he asked mildly, and she realised that she had been staring at him, open-mouthed, with a kind of hunger.

She collected her wits and said, 'I keep doing this to you, don't I? Come in. I'm sorry, I don't know what's the matter with me.'

He followed her into the living room. 'Could it be that you have a lot on your mind lately, some serious things to think about?'

'You've had problems of your own,' she murmured. 'We both need to find ways of dealing with trouble. It's a pity we can't put our heads together and come up with some answers.'

'Perhaps we can,' he said softly. She glanced at him, puzzlement in her expression, but he added, 'I came to offer you moral support. Steve's coming round, isn't he? I thought maybe we could talk to him together.'

'Thanks.' She squeezed his hand gently, then the doorbell sounded again and she went to let Steve in.

She made coffee for all of them to give herself more time, then brought the tray into the living room and set it down on the low table.

Steve came straight to the point. 'Have you decided whether to come with me?' he asked. 'I know it's a difficult decision to make, and I don't want to rush you into anything, but time's running out. If you're not going to come with us then I shall need to find a way to prepare Sophie. She's beginning to understand that I have to work away, and she has some idea of what that means because I was away before Charley died, and she remembers that. I'll always feel guilty about it, and I don't want to let her down. I think she's a bit frightened, though. She keeps asking for you.'

'Might there be an alternative to this?' Daniel asked, and Steve looked at him, a question in his glance.

'Did you have something in mind?'

'Could Sophie stay here? With Emma?'

Emma's heart made a peculiar leap in her chest, and she glanced quickly at Daniel. So he had finally understood what she had tried to tell him. Had he realised she had been thinking along those very same lines? Were their thoughts really so in tune with one another?

Steve frowned. 'But…I shall be away for a long time. This is a permanent job, and I'll need to stay out of the country.'

'I know that. But Sophie loves Emma. I think she could be happy, living here with her.'

'You're asking me to give up my child?'

Daniel pulled in a deep breath. 'It doesn't mean that you would be giving her up. You would still be able to see her when you came home, and Emma could take her to visit with you.'

'Why would you expect me to consider an arrangement like that?'

'Because it would be better for Sophie. She would be able to stay in a country that's familiar to her. She wouldn't be surrounded by strangers, who speak a language she doesn't understand, and if you were sent to other countries—which is on the cards in the type of work you'll be doing—she wouldn't have to be uprooted each time.'

Steve was quiet for a long time, and neither Emma nor Daniel broke the silence. Emma's breath was pent up inside her, waiting for his answer.

Then Steve looked at her and said, 'What do you feel about that?'

She let out the breath. 'I'd like to have Sophie stay here. I think she might be happier on familiar ground. But it has to be your decision…and you would need to be very clear about it because it isn't something that could be chopped and changed as time went on. That would be unsettling for Sophie and it wouldn't be fair on any of us.'

'Are you talking about a formal arrangement, like adoption?'

Emma's heart gave an odd lurch at the enormity of what they were discussing. 'I hadn't thought that far ahead,' she told him honestly, 'but, yes, if it was possible, if you agree to it.'

He was silent, very still, and she was suddenly afraid that he might be put off completely by all this talk.

Steve walked across the room and stared out of the window at the night sky and the dark outlines of the trees. 'You might not be allowed to adopt,' he said quietly, turning around to face her once more. 'You're a single woman and there might be difficulties over that.'

Daniel's glance moved to Emma. 'But not if she were to marry me,' he said.

Emma's eyes widened, but Daniel was looking steadily at Steve now, and Steve said briefly, 'I would want access written into any formal agreement.'

'Are you saying that you'll agree to it?' Emma asked breathlessly. She was bewildered by Daniel's suggestion. He had always seemed to be set against marriage, and now here he was, throwing her emotions into turmoil. She needed to talk to him, find out what he was thinking.

Steve came and rested his hands on her shoulders. 'It's what you want, isn't it, to keep Sophie with you?'

'Yes, it is.' She searched his face, trying to gauge his mood.

'I've tried to do my best by her,' he said, 'but it's hard. I missed so much in the early days, and I sometimes feel that I'm out of my depth. She'll be happy with you, though. I know you'll look after her, and it's what Charley would have wanted. That's what really matters, isn't it?'

'Oh, Steve, what can I say? How can I thank you?'

His mouth made a wry shape. 'Just give me a hug.'

She did just that, and after a while he released her and sent Daniel a long, hard look. 'I thought there was something going on. Sophie keeps talking about you, and the things you've done together.' He frowned. 'You'd better look after both of them. I shall come back at regular intervals and expect to find them both ecstatically happy.'

'I'm sure they will be,' Daniel said. He looked at Emma, and there was a new light in his eyes that filled her with hope for the future.

Steve stayed for about an hour longer. Then he glanced at the clock and said, 'I'd better go and fetch Sophie from the neighbour's house. I expect she'll be full of chatter about the show they've been to see, but once I tell her the news she'll be unstoppable.'

'Give her my love,' Emma said.

'I will.'

After he had gone, Emma went back into the living room and stared up at Daniel, her chest aching with love for him. 'Why have you done this?' she asked him. 'It wasn't what you wanted before.'

'I thought about what you said earlier,' he muttered

thickly. 'You opened my eyes and made me look at the way I've been shutting myself away from everything that's dear to me. I've been unable to trust, afraid to love, because I expected to be hurt again the way I was when my mother left.'

He drew in a deep breath, and went on, 'You were right. I have judged women and found them wanting, until you came into my life like a breath of spring. I told myself you wouldn't stay, you'd move on to better things. I watched you with Sophie and tried to tell myself it wasn't real and the affection you felt was really just born out of duty, that you felt obliged to look after her.'

He shook his head. 'I was wrong, though. You're gentle and caring, everything that I could ever want in a woman. I know that what you feel is love, just as I know that what I feel for you is love. I've been trying to deny it, to tell myself that it doesn't exist, but it's impossible—it's there, and it won't be denied. I love you, Emma.'

She cupped his face with her hands. 'Hold me,' she said, and he gathered her into his arms. 'You don't know how I've longed for you to say that. I've wanted it so badly because I feel the same way about you.'

He captured her mouth, cutting off the flow of words and kissing her with a passionate intensity that took her breath away. She kissed him in return, her heart racing, the blood rushing to her head like strong wine. What seemed like aeons later, when he eventually lifted his head, she said huskily, 'I can't believe this is happening.'

'Believe it,' he murmured. He crushed her to him, and she held onto him as though she would never let him go.

'But you had so many doubts… You said you don't believe in happy ever after…'

His mouth came down on hers, warm and firm, stealing away the words as though he couldn't bear to hear them, and then he groaned raggedly as her lips softened and clung.

'You made me look again at all my preconceived ideas,' he said a little later. 'You made me question my decisions, even to question my relationship with my mother. I had to think again about the way I was reacting to her. Perhaps I should give her a chance to explain. She may not have had too many options, and did what she thought was best.

'I think she was wrong, but we don't have to make the same mistakes, do we? We can be a family. We can support each other, and it will work out for us—I know it will. I love you so much. Will you marry me, Emma? Please? Let me take care of you and Sophie?'

A sob of happiness broke in her throat and she murmured incoherently against the warm curve of his mouth, teasing his lips with her own.

'Was that a yes?' he queried softly.

'Yes. Oh, yes.'

He kissed her again, and she returned his kisses measure for measure, loving him, loving the feel of him, and wanting more, much more. His lips shifted with restless urgency, feverishly gliding over her cheek, her jaw, her throat.

Her hands moved over the broad sweep of his shoulders, and ran along the firm contours of his chest. She was desperate for the touch of his heated skin next to hers, and he must have been driven by the same compelling need because somehow they ended up in her bedroom, sinking down on the bed, their limbs tangling on the soft quilt, their clothes lying rumpled on the floor.

Emma's heart was thudding wildly as he looked down at her. 'You're lovely,' he whispered. 'In body and soul.'

His hands caressed her, following a questing, sensual path, discovering every gentle curve and smooth plane, and lingering tantalisingly on her silken flesh until the excitement was almost more than she could bear. His lips followed the trail of his hands with a teasing intimacy that awoke her body to a feverish, tormented desire.

She arched her spine restlessly, hunger throbbing deep within her. Soft cries of need broke in her throat, and she felt him move over her, the lean strength of his thighs nudging hers. His hands lifted her gently, tenderly, to him, and when he possessed her completely and utterly, she caught her breath with the intensity of the consuming flame that surged through her whole body.

She followed the rhythm of his movement as though their bodies had been in tune with each other since time began. The rhythm built to a powerful crescendo and then sensation exploded in her, and in the long aftermath ripples of exquisite pleasure flowed through her. Daniel's muffled groan of satisfaction echoed her own.

He held her close, and she savoured the feel of his powerful male body against hers. His heart thudded reassuringly beneath her cheek.

'I feel as though I've come home after a long, long journey,' she said softly.

'And so you have,' he murmured. 'We've both come home, to each other.'

MILLS & BOON®

Makes
any time
special

Copyright © Harlequin Enterprises Limited 1997
All rights reserved

Enjoy a romantic novel from
Mills & Boon®

Presents...™ *Enchanted*™ TEMPTATION.

Historical Romance™ ✛ MEDICAL
ROMANCE

MILLS & BOON®

MEDICAL ROMANCE™

A FAMILIAR FEELING by Margaret Barker

Dr Caroline Bennett found working at the Chateau Clinique with Pierre, the boy she'd adored as a child, wasn't easy. It didn't help that his ex-wife was still around.

HEART IN HIDING by Jean Evans

Dr Holly Hunter needed respite, and the remote Scottish village was ideal. Until Callum McLoud turned up accusing her of treating his patients!

HIS MADE-TO-ORDER BRIDE by Jessica Matthews
Bachelor Doctors

Dr J.D. Berkely had a good job in ER, a delightful son Daniel, and a truly good friend in nurse Katie Alexander, so why would he need a wife?

A TIMELY AFFAIR by Helen Shelton

Dr Merrin Ryan sees that widowed Professor Neil McAlister needs nurturing and she falls in love! But Neil is aware that he could damage her career…

Available from 5th November 1999

Available at most branches of WH Smith, Tesco, Martins, Borders, Easons, Volume One/James Thin and most good paperback bookshops

COMING NEXT MONTH

MILLS & BOON®

Presents...™

MARRIAGE ULTIMATUM *by Lindsay Armstrong*

Neve couldn't work out why Rob Stowe was suddenly insisting upon marrying her, or whether she should even say 'yes' when the mother of his child was still so much in evidence!

MISTRESS BY ARRANGEMENT *by Helen Bianchin*

Nikos Alessandros needed a social hostess and Michelle needed a male companion to deter an unwanted suitor. A convenient affair—if they can keep their passions in check!

BARTALDI'S BRIDE *by Sara Craven*

Guido Bartaldi had obviously decided upon his reluctant ward as his wife. When Clare accepted a position with him she began to suspect that Guido had an entirely different set of intentions!

BOUGHT: ONE HUSBAND *by Diana Hamilton*

In her innocence Alissa offered to pay Jethro Cole to marry her, to comply with the conditions of her uncle's will. In fact Jethro was a millionaire intent on making Alissa his own.

Available from 5th November 1999

Available at most branches of WH Smith, Tesco, Martins, Borders, Easons, Volume One/James Thin and most good paperback bookshops

COMING NEXT MONTH

MILLS & BOON®

Presents...™

THE SOCIETY GROOM by *Mary Lyons*
(Society Weddings)

Once, they'd had a passionate affair. When they met again at a society wedding Olivia thought she'd lost all interest in Dominic FitzCharles—until he made a surprise announcement…

SLADE BARON'S BRIDE by *Sandra Marton*
(The Barons)

When Lara Stevens met Slade Baron an overnight flight delay led to a tempting invitation. Who would Lara hurt if she accepted? He wanted her and she wanted…a baby.

GIBSON'S GIRL by *Anne McAllister*

Gibson was fascinated by the shy and beautiful Chloe. Should he seduce her? Gib was tempted. Should she resist him? Chloe had to. Eventually it became a question of who was seducing whom!

MARRIAGE ON TRIAL by *Lee Wilkinson*

Elizabeth had insisted on an annulment - and disappeared from Quinn's life. Now he'd tracked her down and claimed she was still his wife. Did he really love her, or did he want revenge?

Available from 5th November 1999

Available at most branches of WH Smith, Tesco, Martins, Borders, Easons, Volume One/James Thin and most good paperback bookshops

2 FREE

books and a surprise gift!

We would like to take this opportunity to thank you for reading this Mills & Boon® book by offering you the chance to take TWO more specially selected titles from the Medical Romance™ series absolutely FREE! We're also making this offer to introduce you to the benefits of the Reader Service™—

- ★ FREE home delivery
- ★ FREE gifts and competitions
- ★ FREE monthly Newsletter
- ★ Exclusive Reader Service discounts
- ★ Books available before they're in the shops

Accepting these FREE books and gift places you under no obligation to buy, you may cancel at any time, even after receiving your free shipment. Simply complete your details below and return the entire page to the address below. *You don't even need a stamp!*

YES! Please send me 2 free Medical Romance books and a surprise gift. I understand that unless you hear from me, I will receive 4 superb new titles every month for just £2.40 each, postage and packing free. I am under no obligation to purchase any books and may cancel my subscription at any time. The free books and gift will be mine to keep in any case.

M9EA

Ms/Mrs/Miss/Mr ....Initials...............................
BLOCK CAPITALS PLEASE

Surname ....

Address ....

....

....Postcode...............................

Send this whole page to:
UK: FREEPOST CN81, Croydon, CR9 3WZ
EIRE: PO Box 4546, Kilcock, County Kildare (stamp required)

Offer valid in UK and Eire only and not available to current Reader Service subscribers to this series. We reserve the right to refuse an application and applicants must be aged 18 years or over. Only one application per household. Terms and prices subject to change without notice. Offer expires 30th April 2000. As a result of this application, you may receive further offers from Harlequin Mills & Boon and other carefully selected companies. If you would prefer not to share in this opportunity please write to The Data Manager at the address above.

Mills & Boon is a registered trademark owned by Harlequin Mills & Boon Limited.
Medical Romance is being used as a trademark.

THE Regency COLLECTION

Where rogues find romance

Look out for the seventh volume in this limited collection of Regency Romances from Mills & Boon® in November.

Featuring:

The Cyprian's Sister
by Paula Marshall

and

A Compromised Lady
by Francesca Shaw

Still only £4.99

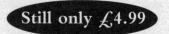

MILLS & BOON®

Makes any time special™

Available at most branches of WH Smith, Tesco, Martins, Borders, Easons, Volume One / James Thin and most good paperback bookshops